GYPSI

CW00539247

JANTAR CLASSICS

GYPSIES

BY KAREL HYNEK MÁCHA

Translated from the Czech,
with an introduction,
by Geoffrey Chew

JANTAR PUBLISHING

London 2019

First published in Great Britain in 2019 by
Jantar Publishing Ltd
www.jantarpublishing.com

Originally published as *Cikáni: Román pozůstalých spisů Karla Hynka Máchy* (Prague: K. Jeřábková, 1857)

A CIP catalogue record for this book is available from the British Library
ISBN 978-0-9934467-6-4

This translation was made possible by a grant from
the Ministry of Culture of the Czech Republic

MINISTRY OF CULTURE
CZECH REPUBLIC

For Czech friends, old and new

CONTENTS

NOTE ON THE TRANSLATION

THE TEXT OF THE NOVEL is taken from the standard modern edition, in Karel Hynek Mácha, *Prózy* [*Prose Works*], edited by Zdeněk Hrbata, Martin Procházka, and Martin Stluka (Prague: Lidové noviny, 2008), pp. 171–275. To the best of my knowledge, there have been no earlier translations of this novel into English, except that translations of the closing passages of Chapters 13 and 15 were appended to Hugh Hamilton McGoverne's English translation of Mácha's *May* (Prague: Orbis, 1949). The names of the characters in this translation are those of the original, except that I have anglicized the spellings of some (Leah, Judith). Generally I have attempted to strike a balance between readability and period vocabulary. For the embedded poems (the songs sung by the young Gypsy, Leah, and Angelina, in Chapters 2, 3, and 4), I have roughly adopted the metres and rhyme-schemes of Mácha's original, and I hope that the resulting reminiscence of Longfellow's *Hiawatha* in the Nagy-Ida song in Chapter 3 will not seem out of place.

The extended, mock-scholarly, footnote in Chapter 3, concerning the siege of Nagy-Ida in the sixteenth century, and its defence by Gypsies, is Mácha's own, and draws (without acknowledgment) on a story about it that is told in the treatise on the Gypsies by Heinrich Grellmann that is further discussed below in the Introduction, and in several other sources of the eighteenth and early nineteenth centuries.

Each chapter of the novel is headed by quotations in Polish from epics, plays, and verses, recently published, which Mácha is known to have been reading at the time he was writing. I have translated these and have added the titles and dates of their sources, and have restored the original English for the extracts from Moore and Byron, heading Chapter 3, which are quoted by Mácha in the Polish transla-tions of Julian Korsak (1807–55). These quotations closely echo many of the characters and situations in the novel, sometimes literally and sometimes with ironic effect. For a modern reader likely to be unfamiliar with the Polish sources, they will inevitably lose much of their rhetorical force, but one must wonder what even a nineteenth-century Czech reading public could have made of them. Perhaps Mácha was playing a private game, setting riddles to fire, or tax, the imagination of his readers, or using them as tesserae to build an allusive narrative mosaic of his own.

For Bárta's comic malapropisms in Chapter 9, I have attempted to provide equivalents, in view of the impossibility of direct translations. In his conversation with the clerks carrying torches, Bárta claims to have been a 'light' himself since his schooldays. First he thinks the term 'parva' (the lowest class in a Gymnasium) means 'barva', Czech for 'colour'. Next he misremembers his German teacher calling him 'dumm', stupid, and reports that the word was 'dummen', and meant a light; meanwhile, the clerks are laughingly suggesting that the teacher must have been using Latin, and calling him a 'lumen'. I hope that the English word-play I have introduced goes some way towards creating an equivalent effect.

My thanks are due in particular to Moray Comrie, for supplying the cover art; to Agnieszka Budzińska-Bennett, for advice on the translation of the Polish quotations; and to colleagues and friends who have discussed this text, and my Introduction to it, with me, especially Jonathan Bellman, of the University of Northern Colorado, Peter Zusi, of the School of Slavonic and East European Studies (SSEES), University College London, and the always stimulating participants in the Czech Literature seminar at SSEES; but I bear full responsibility for the results.

INTRODUCTION

ANY ACCOUNT of the work of Karel Hynek Mácha, for a general English-speaking readership, ought to begin with his reputation, for he is widely regarded today as the effective founder of modern Czech poetry and literature, and as by far the greatest figure of literary Czech High Romanticism. Born in Prague on 16 November 1810, the son of a tradesman, he studied law at Prague University, and participated actively in the theatrical and political life of the Bohemian capital, avidly following contemporary literary developments in Czech, German, and Polish; he also read English texts in German and Polish translation. Shortly after taking up a position in a law firm at Litoměřice [Leitmeritz], in 1836, he contracted an infection after helping in fighting a fire, and he died there on 6 November 1836; in his premature death, European literary culture lost a prodigy of astonishing promise.

Macha's own work includes poems, prose, and fragments of plays, but his reputation rests principally on a single work, his *chef-d'œuvre*, the verse epic, *May [Máj]* (1836). The general context of his work is, broadly, Byronic Romanticism, as it was also of Polish Romantic writing of the period: in the 1840s, the eminent Polish poet Adam Mickiewicz called Byron a 'mysterious link, joining the great Slavonic literature with the literature of Western Europe'.[1] But for Mácha this was initially an obstacle to recognition and acceptance, for Bohemian Byronists were mistrusted and subject at times to Austrian police surveillance.

In any case, some Bohemian patriots at first thought Byron's 'frenetic' writing unsuitable as a literary model for the Czech National Revival, preferring the simplicity of folk-song, and the stirring deeds of an imagined heroic national past. In fact Mácha's reputation was not consolidated until the late 1850s, many years after his death, when the so-called 'Májovci', a group naming themselves and their yearbook after *May*, set that poem up as a literary model. *May* eventually became established as a centrally important reference point in nearly all new developments in Czech literature, including twentieth-century avant-gardism. It was never challenged even under Communism, and generations of Czech schoolchildren were given its opening lines to memorize.

On the surface, these opening lines merely seem a stereotyped invocation of Romanticism. They summon Nature to love, one idyllic May evening, in language of great beauty. But they already hint at complexities, and the poem soon reveals that this beauty, this love, and indeed any notion of a purpose to human existence, are nothing but falsehoods and lies. In the words of Martin Procházka, 'all the charms of spring are represented in the poem only to obscure the sense of nothingness, namely the general absence of purpose in the universe'.[2] Vilém, the hero, in a variant of the Oedipus myth, has killed his father, the seducer of his betrothed; not only is he executed for this crime, but this happens without mitigation, and without any hope of an apotheosis or an afterlife in which he might be reunited with his beloved Jarmila.

Gypsies [*Cikáni*], the present novel, is in many ways a companion piece to this poem. It was written in 1835, the year before *May*, but (as Mácha complained, in a letter written in late January or early February 1836) the censors prohibited its publication, 'no one knows why'. Chapters 1–7 first appeared in the periodical *Lumír* in 1851, and the whole novel was not published until 1857. No complete autograph MS survives, and doubts were raised about its authorship in the 1950s and 1960s, but these are now generally dismissed as groundless.[3]

A Novel of Lies and Deception

Gypsies shares the underlying nihilism of *May*, as is immediately suggested by the motto preceding Chapter 1, 'Long my journey, / a vain quest', which it shares with *May*. It resembles *May* in several other respects as well, but particularly in the motif of deception. Lies become a controlling theme in it: this Gothic narrative is ostensibly reaching out to uncover identity – of mysterious strangers, of rapists and murderers, even of national origins – but at every point it resists truthful answers to such questions.

In this tale, two wandering Gypsies arrive, unannounced and apparently by chance, in exotic, foreign dress, in a curious settlement of scattered houses.[4] The location is simultaneously familiar and alien. It is introduced as a primevally, authentically Czech landscape, lying in a deep valley, which in an echo of Genesis has emerged from a chaos of endless waters. So a reader may expect the theme of ancient national continuity to be developed. But this landscape provides no consolation. It is hostile and forbidding, seemingly Oriental, complete with ruined castle and terrifying forests and precipices, and very hard for a reader to visualize, despite the meticulous description, which is probably based on the castle of Kokořín.[5] None the less, it seems unaccountably familiar to the Gypsies, though their origins are unknown, and dreadful traumas seem to lie in its past as also in theirs.

But there are repeated hints from the outset that any, or all, details of the story may be untrue, and a key role is played by Bárta, the only main character who is unquestionably Czech. He is a superstitious, ill-educated, loquacious veteran of the Napoleonic wars, and is nicknamed 'Flacon' on account of his perpetual drunkenness. It was long ago suggested that Mácha might have modelled him on the bibulous and garrulous Corporal Jacob Bunting in Edward Lytton Bulwer's tiresome *Eugene Aram* (1831), another novel of mysterious strangers and of murder.[6] Fortunately, however, he has been completely recast, if so. Bárta is a supremely gifted story-teller, from whom the first-person narrator has apparently received the whole of this tale; his narration is absurdly, and comically, packed with transparent lies and exaggerations. Just the same, he is the only character to achieve good fortune. At the end, he has gained not only the tenancy of the single inn in this landscape, but also a new annual subsidy from the castle. It might be a pessimistic modern parable. It is only a comprehensively unreliable liar who is able to tell this tale, and benefit from it.

As the dreamlike narrative progresses, the characters seem increasingly haunted by ancient crimes; and when the local Count in this landscape, Valdemar of Bork, is finally murdered, it seems that these earlier crimes may hold clues to the identity of the murderer. Indeed *Gypsies* has something of the structure of a murder mystery, with such clues constantly being dropped in the narrative. Perhaps the older Gypsy really is a former Venetian gondolier, seeking vengeance for the kidnap and seduction of his mistress by an anonymous young foreigner; perhaps this foreigner really was Valdemar; perhaps Valdemar really is a satyromaniac, responsible for the rape and ruin of most of the female characters in the novel, in sex orgies in his castle that have unhinged his victims and have rendered them, too, entirely unreliable as witnesses. The young Gypsy at first seems to be the son, or the adoptive son, of the old one, but neither of them is apparently Gypsy by birth. He combines physical beauty with some strange deformities. These include a distinctive birthmark, a motif which will make any reader suspect that the plot will turn on *anagnorisis*, in the sense that Aristotle gives the word in the *Poetics*, especially in Chapter 16 of that text: 'recognition', the turning-point in a drama at which the characters move from ignorance and confusion to reliable knowledge and understanding, identities are established, and the plot is resolved. So some older Czech criticism has proceeded on the assumption that the mysteries are resolved at the point when the perpetrators of its crimes are recognized as Valdemar and the old Gypsy, their motives are recognized as desire for revenge and jealousy, and the young Gypsy is recognized as the long-lost son of Valdemar.[7]

But the novel is unsatisfactory, and indeed trivialized, if read in that way. There are several recognition scenes, and *anagnorisis* is repeatedly hinted at. Yet none of these scenes provides the rational unravelling of clues that would be necessary to achieve closure, and all are strange: lies and false leads are never satisfactorily replaced by truth. Near the beginning, in Chapter 2, is the scene with songs of exile sung by the Gypsies and by Leah, the daughter of the Jewish innkeeper. These songs suggest an affinity between Jews and Gypsies, as comrades in exile among strangers, both 'nations' equally deprived of a fatherland. They provoke intense mutual recognition, which seems deeply convincing and moving, and even the old Jewish innkeeper is reduced to tears. But the essential implausibility of the scene is highlighted in the ensuing internal struggle of the elderly Jew at the prospect of his fortune passing to the young Gypsy, a total stranger.

Another, curious, approach to recognition is taken in the scene of the initial conversation between the young Gypsy and Bárta, also in Chapter 2, where a reader must suspect that a recognition scene is being set up. Bárta speaks of a mysterious four-year-old boy, with physical deformities, whom he had met 17 years earlier, and of a mysterious son allegedly borne by the Countess, 22 years earlier, also with these deformities. And the Gypsy he is addressing is a young man in his twenties, again with the same deformities, who says he passed by at the age of four. The Gypsy seems deeply affected by the interchange; yet neither the drunk Bárta nor the sober Gypsy remarks explicitly on the arithmetical coincidences, and nothing is made of them. The scene simply relapses into dream-like silence, as Bárta disappears into the landscape. Later recognition scenes turn on the discovery of supposedly authentic documents in unlikely locations, or by the too sudden recognition of physical attributes. They too are essentially implausible, and yet their consequences are increasingly far-reaching. The murder of Valdemar is investigated; the young Gypsy is suddenly exonerated, and the old Gypsy is equally suddenly hanged, as the murderer, in both cases to the acclaim of the rabble, but on transparently inadequate evidence in both cases. Equally, no convincingly solid evidence is offered when the young Gypsy is suddenly acclaimed in Chapter 13 as Valdemar's true son and heir.

Now it is true, as Terence Cave remarks in his study of the trope, that *anagnorisis* is by its very nature implausible, often amounting to 'a shoddy way of resolving a plot the author can no longer control', and that it is easily parodied.[8] But here it seems that the device is being used neither in the conventional manner nor in parody, but rather against itself, to construct *reductiones ad absurdum*, and thereby to dismantle identities. In consequence, the reader is denied the consolation of any rational explanation, and of any happy – or even tragic – ending. Nothing, it seems, has real meaning, and nothing can ever be fully explicable.

The extreme is reached in two later scenes. At the point when the supposed last will and testament of the murdered Count is read out, a reader might expect the young Gypsy's true identity to have been established finally and firmly. Instead, the reader is presented with an astonishing virtuoso expression of irrationality. The young Gypsy, with only an adoptive father (the old Gypsy) at the beginning of the narrative, has dreamt of searching for his real mother in Chapter 5. That dream is likely to have set up the expectation that he will find her, even if perhaps merely in recognizing his true native land. But pseudo-recognitions have ensued, in which he has been presented successively with two supposedly true mothers (Angelina, the madwoman, and Emma, the Countess); and now with a supposedly true father (Valdemar). There is an overload of information; the dream of the lost mother is forgotten, and he is unhinged, abandoning reason altogether. This is the surreal passage, at the end of Chapter 12, that has most frequently been quoted by critics, and in the twentieth century it served as a model for the 'automatic' writing of the avant-garde Czech 'Poetists' before World War II:

> Under his breath [the young Gypsy] whispered, devoid of memory, oblivious of the sense of the individual words: 'My father! – my father seduced my mother – no, he murdered my mother – by my mother – no, he seduced my mistress by my mother – he seduced the mistress of my father – seduced my mother – and my father murdered my father!'

Towards the end of the novel, in Chapter 13, recognition and reconciliation are thwarted more radically still, and with them, notions of innocence and guilt, in what is perhaps its most disturbing scene of all. The old Gypsy is left alone with the young one, an hour before his execution. Superfluously and arbitrarily, he begs the young Gypsy for forgiveness. Brutally, and without explanation, the young Gypsy remains completely silent, as both Gypsies had remained during most of the murder investigation. There is no gesture of human sympathy, let alone any reconciliation with any expression of emotion, to break the shocking silence; and we are left permanently ignorant of the 'real' relationship between the two men, or of the guilt or innocence of either of them, if indeed any of these has had any meaning at all.

And at a period when national self-awareness was a central issue for patriots, this nihilism has remarkable further consequences for Mácha's exploration of national identity in this text, even though he is ostensibly drawing heavily on stereotypes and earlier models for his characterization of the 'nations' of the Gypsies and the Jews, and of the Bohemian aristocracy. A few of these models may be mentioned.

As for the Gypsies, Mácha, like every other writer in Europe at this period, does not escape the influence of Heinrich Grellmann, the 'armchair anthropologist' who had published a treatise on the Roma in 1783 (2nd edition, 1787).[9] Grellmann rebuts their supposed Egyptian origins, and recognizes their connection with India, while essentializing their Oriental origins, and dwelling on their aesthetic and sensual beauty, and their artistic talent, as well as their lack of civilization and their untrustworthiness. For the Gypsies Mácha may also be drawing on Alexander Pushkin's verse narrative, *The Gypsies* [*Tsygany*] (published in 1827). He is known to have read an anonymous English critique of Pushkin (first published in the *Foreign Quarterly Review* in 1832) in German translation in January 1833: among other works, the critic praises *The Gypsies* in this article, despite the opinion that 'there is certainly not much in the subject to repay curiosity', for the heightened dramatic effect of the passages with dialogue set out under the names of the characters, as in a play text.[10] Mácha does the latter, unexpectedly and less consistently, at the moment of most intense conflict in Chapter 6. And the picture of the old Gypsy, 'sitting, alone, warmed by the last heat of the fire', in the letter at the end of Chapter 14, is a near-quotation from Pushkin's 'Inside his tent an old man remains awake, / he sits in front of the embers, / warmed by their last heat, / and gazes into the distance / wrapped in nocturnal mists.'[11]

Mácha's stereotypes also include the pious but rapacious Jewish innkeeper amassing a fortune by exploiting his Gentile Czech clientele, who is a regrettable stock figure in Czech fiction. In conformity with literary stereotype, the Jew has only a daughter, Leah, and no sons, even though this is no normal 'conversion' narrative; however, Leah's exile song in Chapter 2 also has obvious prototypes in some of Byron's *Hebrew Melodies* of 1815, which began to be published in Czech translation from 1823.[12] The Orientalism of Czech Jewry, and the pathos of homelessness, together with aspirations to rooted Czech identity, are found even in poetry by Czech Jews themselves, such as Sigfrid Kapper's slightly later *Czech Pages* [*České listy*] of 1846.[13] And the aristocratic libertinism of Valdemar, the local nobleman, draws on well-known eighteenth-century stereotypes.

So a reader of the period would have recognized familiar stereotypes, and would no doubt have expected them to be deployed in familiar ways. But no such thing happens. The notion of the 'Bohemian' is invoked in a manner that is far from patriotic, drawing on the old senses of the words 'Bohemian' and 'bohémien', with reference to Gypsies, and resisting any form of national categorization, though conflating them with the word 'Bohemian' in its geographical sense. This is the case even though the Czech word for Gypsy does not admit this ambiguity: it is 'cikán', that is, *tzigane*, and pronounced in almost the same way. Besides Byron, one of the points of contact between this novel and earlier literature in western Europe is the novels of Walter Scott. And Hayraddin, the 'Bohemian' in the fifteenth-century French setting of Walter Scott's *Quentin Durward* (1823), is a nomadic Gypsy in this sense: he insists that he is of no country, and that he is 'a Zingaro, a Bohemian, an Egyptian, or whatever the Europeans, in their different languages, may chuse to call our people'.[14] In Mácha's *Gypsies*, Scott's vague conflation of Bohemians, Czechs, Egyptians, and Gypsies, not only remains unresolved, but is expanded at the outset to include Hungarians: Mácha's own reading included the Austrian painter F. S. Chrismar's *Skizzen einer Reise durch Ungarn in die Türkei* (1834), and Chrismar's chapter on the Hungarian Gypsies, though heavily dependent on Grellmann, may have suggested some aspects of the description of the young Gypsy and his Hungarian costume in Chapter 2.[15]

Whether or not the young Gypsy can be identified correctly as Bohemian – Czech – by birth, the end of the novel shows that vagabondage and homelessness remain his natural qualities. They may in fact be the best means of proving him a true Bohemian – but, if so, with the ineradicable possibility that he is as untrustworthy and deceitful as is this entire narrative. And, far from their being the pure, heroic nation imagined by patriots, the Bohemians, understood in this sense, have in any case been described by the young Gypsy in Chapter 12 as a society completely free of conventional group loyalties, 'a motley crowd in strange confusion', for whom origins and racial identity are so unimportant that 'a puppy is suckled at a sow's breast, a piglet at the udder of a bitch'.

Music and Language

These questions of national identity reach a further dimension in Mácha's handling of music and language, neither of which is treated in a remotely realistic manner, and both of which suggest an interest in Hegel, which is well-documented for Mácha and prompted criticism of him from contemporaries (although it is not certain that Mácha read Hegel's own writings rather than those of his disciples, and Mácha clearly did not share Hegel's views on Christianity or indeed religion in general).[16] As for music, the young Gypsy introduces himself with a conventionally Romantic lyric song in Chapter 2, and then with an epic, the Nagy-Ida song, in Chapter 3. Embedded within the narrative, these songs, and especially the epic, should suffice in Hegel's terms to characterize the claim of the Gypsies to nationhood. Hegel puts the matter thus:

> Since the epic has 'what is' as its topic, it acquires as its object the occurrence of an action which in the full breadth of its circumstances and relationships must gain access to our contemplation as a rich event connected with the entire world of a nation and epoch ... As such an original totality, the epic is the saga, the book, the Bible of a people, and every great and important nation has its absolutely earliest books of this type, in which that which is its own original spirit is articulated to it.[17]

So the presence of a epic is essential to the legitimacy of any national literature; and the development of Greek literature from Homeric epic to lyric provides a model for the development of every subsequent vernacular literature. Mácha further invites the reader to understand the Nagy-Ida song in this way, by inserting his footnote in Chapter 3. And with deep irony he refers the epic to a legend about the Gypsies that may have been the most ancient one current at the time, that is quoted by Grellmann in his treatise on the Gypsies, already mentioned, from the much earlier work of the Hungarian Jesuit László Turóczi.[18] The episode it narrates was claimed to have occurred in the sixteenth century at the stronghold of Nagy-Ida (now Veľká Ida, south of Košice in eastern Slovakia), which was formerly held by the Perényi family, and involved the defence of the stronghold by Gypsies. The defence was initially successful, but the episode ended with all the Gypsies slaughtered owing to their boastful stupidity. More recently it has been claimed that Mácha's Nagy-Ida epic song itself corresponds to an ancient traditional Roma lament, 'Fároe, fároe, kherdeczina phengoe', perhaps relating to this tragedy, that survived into the twentieth century at least.[19] I have not attempted to verify this claim, nor to prove or disprove the historicity of any of the details of the Nagy-Ida legend. Whatever basis any of them may have in historical fact, however, the song palpably fails to meet Hegel's standard, for the deeds commemorated in it are the opposite of heroic, and in other ways, too, the song torpedoes any notion that the Gypsies might be a nation entitled to their own territory.

Nevertheless, in a strange sleight of hand, in the novel this song becomes a universal epic of permanent exile. It provides the stimulus for the instinctive sympathy between Gypsy and Jew that follows. But it also reaches out to define the affinity of both Gypsy and Jew with the Bohemians, whether or not understood as Czechs (though the traditional claim to superlative musicality for the Bohemians, since the eighteenth century, is strangely passed over here), and to provide the illusion of a surrogate homeland, perhaps only temporary, for all of them in this Orientalized Czech heartland. Moreover, in a Baroque conceit, the landscape itself participates in this instinctive sympathy: strange, harmonious music, and strange, bewitching perfumes, emanate from it, without any human agency.

So one might read this Jewish-Gypsy alliance as a further radical rejection of an exclusively Czech, settled, patriotism, particularly when the young Gypsy, now unexpectedly (and very temporarily) reconciled to abandoning his wandering, and settling with Leah, declares, near the end of Chapter 5. 'Zde domov můj', 'Here is my homeland'. This is a near-quotation from a song embedded in Josef Kajetán Tyl's patriotic play *Fidlovačka*, which had been premiered in Prague in December 1834, only months before Mácha wrote *Gypsies*; the first words of the song are 'Kde domov můj?', 'Where is my homeland?'.[20] (This song, in its setting by František Škroup (1860), later became the Czech national anthem, and the quotation is therefore no doubt even more resonant for modern Czech readers than it can have been in 1835.)

It is instructive to compare this account of Mácha's with the later, much more familiar, definition of Gypsy music by the composer Franz Liszt, in his *Des Bohémiens et de leur musique en Hongrie* (1859).[21] Liszt, or whoever was responsible for this part of his text, also constructs an account of Gypsy epic, claiming that it is embodied in his own Hungarian Rhapsodies, and he draws explicitly on Hegel's theory of the epic in order to do so, as Nicholas Saul has emphasized.[22] But Liszt's reading of Hegel is new, and creates a stable notion of Gypsy identity, entirely opposed to that of Mácha. Moreover, he claims that this is completely irreconcilable with Jewish identity in almost every respect, including music. In this, both Gypsy and Jewish identity entirely lose the fluidity they possess in Mácha: they become fixed, and indeed racialized (increasingly so, in later editions).

For Mácha, music is only a metaphor: unlike Liszt among others, he is entirely unconcerned about the ways in which the music of the Gypsies, or of the Jews, might be realized in actual practice. But language is of central import to him, not least because it is in his work that the literary Czech language is first coming to birth in its modern form. Yet it, too, is treated with extraordinary, dreamlike reticence and restraint. Through most of the novel, it is entirely unclear what language the characters are speaking in order to communicate with each other. Realistically, the setting of the novel would be a linguistic Babel. German cannot be the lingua franca of the characters, for we learn from his malapropisms in Chapter 9 that Bárta is a monoglot Czech, unable to communicate in German, and without the faintest understanding of what he had been told in that language at school. The old Gypsy and Angelina are both allegedly Italians from Venice, and the old Gypsy is allegedly a complete stranger in the locality. The young Gypsy arrives muttering words in a strange language, which might, or might not, be Romani. Leah and her father presumably speak Yiddish or German; the court officials in later chapters must speak German. And language, as a badge of nationality, would be expected to take a central place for an author contributing to the National Revival. Yet linguistic confrontation is absent: both Gypsies are instantly able to converse with Bárta, none of the characters seems to speak with a foreign accent, and they all understand one another's speech. And, as with the music, the landscape understands, too, with the rocks returning meaningful echoes of their utterances. It is the sort of understanding that exists only in dreams, and never touches their essential identities. So the narrative not only undermines personal and group identity, but, more radically still, also suggests that these scarcely exist at all.

All these features may well have seemed disadvantages from the point of view of National Revivalists contemporary with Mácha, with their concerns for patriotism and ideological purity, and no doubt contributed to the relative neglect of Mácha's poetry by Czech composers seeking texts to set to music. (There have nevertheless been several dramatizations of both *May* and *Gypsies*, with music, and *Gypsies* was recast as a movie, directed by Karl Anton, in 1922.) But modern readers have different interests, and may find better rewards in the mysterious depths of this tale. Its refusal to short-circuit the complications of personal identity, group loyalties, and national self-identification, may well be a reason why Mácha has found increasing favour since the 1850s, and even why his writings now take a central place in the Czech literary canon. His mysterious avoidance of patriotic cliché may suit his work also to the tastes of readers for whom he is not a familiar canonic figure; and indeed an English translation of the present text seems long overdue.

Egham, January 2019

NOTES TO INTRODUCTION

1 'Byron jest tajemniczem ogniwem, łączącem wielką literaturę słowiańską z literaturą zachodniej Europy', quoted from a lecture Mickiewicz gave in Paris at the Sorbonne, in Mirosława Modrzewska, 'Pilgrimage or Revolt?: The Dilemmas of Polish Byronism', *The Reception of Byron in Europe*, vol. 2 (*Northern, Central, and Eastern Europe*), ed. Richard A. Cardwell (London & New York: Thoemmes Continuum, 2004), pp. 305–15, at p. 307.

2 Martin Procházka, 'Byron in Czech Culture', in *The Reception of Byron in Europe*, vol. 2 (London & New York, 2004), p. 295 n. 23.

3 The circumstances of the genesis of the novel, including suggestions for some of the sources of its motifs, are outlined in Martin Stluka, ed., *Karel Hynek Mácha: Prózy [Mácha: Prose Works]* (Prague: Lidové noviny, 2008), pp. 445–66.

4 It may be necessary to point out that the word 'Gypsy' in this text, and in the title of the novel, is not an accurate or appropriate term when used to refer to the Roma or Sinti people to whom it has often been applied, either historically or at the present day. But this novel, and most of the other eighteenth- and nineteenth-century texts quoted here, are far from being works of ethnography, and their 'Gypsies' should best be understood as purely literary motifs.

5 Much of the topography described in the novel is doubtless based on personal observation by Mácha in his repeated *Fusswanderungen* through Bohemia and through Europe. A drawing of Kokořín by Mácha survives, and this dependence on personal experience seems likely particularly in the descriptions of places in and around the Gulfs of Venice and Trieste in the letter of the old Gypsy in Chapter 14, for Mácha's travels included a journey on foot from Prague to Venice.

6   Vojtěch Jirát, 'Čtenář Bulwera' [Mácha, Reader of Lytton Bulwer], in Karel Janský and Vojtěch Jirát, *Tajemství Křivokladu a jiné máchovské studie* [*The Mystery of [Mácha's] Křivoklad, and Other Mácha Studies*] (Prague: Václav Petr, 1941). Bulwer was the surname of the novelist and politician until 1843, when he changed it by royal licence to Bulwer Lytton. – Bárta is characterized by Doležel as 'not a fictional character in the true sense of the word: he is a schematic figure personifying an unreliable narrator' ('Bárta není v pravém slova smyslu fikční osoba, je to schematická figurka zosobňující nespolehlivého vypravěče', Lubomír Doležel, 'Dva fikční světy trpnosti: Máchovi Cikáni a Zeyerův Dům "U tonoucí hvězdy"' [Two Fictional Worlds of Passivity: Mácha's *Gypsies* and Zeyer's *The House of the Sinking Star*], in Aleš Haman and Radim Kopáč, eds., *Mácha redivivus (1810–2010): sborník ke dvoustému výročí narození Karla Hynka Máchy* [*Mácha Redivivus: Festschrift for the Bicentenary of the Birth of Mácha*] (Prague: Academia, 2010), pp. 422–40, here at p. 426.

7   Cf. the summary of the plot offered in Marie Hrubešová, *Máchovy výrazové prostředky k charakteristice osob v románu "Cikáni" / Les moyens d'expression de Mácha en tant que caractéristique des personnages de son roman "Cikáni"* (Prague: Universita Karlova, 1936), p. 71.

8   Terence Cave, *Recognitions: A Study in Poetics* (Oxford, UK: Clarendon Press, 1988), p. 1.

9   Heinrich Moritz Gottlieb Grellmann, *Historischer Versuch über die Zigeuner betreffend die Lebensart und Verfassung Sitten und Schicksale dieses Volks seit seiner Erscheinung in Europa, und dessen Ursprung* (1st ed., Dessau and Leipzig: Auf Kosten der Verlags-Kasse, 1783; 2nd ed., Göttingen: Johann Christian Dieterich, 1787).

10 *The Foreign Quarterly Review*, vol. 9 (London: Treuttel and Würtz and Richter/Black, Young and Young, January and May 1832), pp. 398–418. On Pushkin's *Poltava* (1829), the reviewer remarks,

'By many of his countrymen, Pushkin has been styled the Russian Byron – an appellation too flattering, if meant to imply poetical powers and energy equal to those of the English bard' (p. 398). The critique of *The Gypsies* (pp. 408–10) draws attention to several motifs also relevant to Mácha's *Gypsies*, including murders motivated by extreme jealousy, and guilt that is not accompanied by remorse.

11 Aleksandr Sergeevich Pushkin, *Tsygany* [*The Gypsies*], lines 26–31:

> В шатре одном старик не спит;
> Он перед углями сидит,
> Согретый их последним жаром,
> И в поле дальнее глядит,
> Ночным подернутое паром.
> Его молоденькая дочь
> Пошла гулять в пустынном поле.

(In A. S. Pushkin, *Sobranie sochinenii v desiati tomakh* [*Collected Works in Ten Volumes*], Moscow: Khudozhestvennaya literatura, 1975, vol. 3, p. 152.)

12 George Gordon, Lord Byron, *Hebrew Melodies* (London: John Murray, 1815).

13 Sigfrid Kapper, *České listy* [*Czech Pages*] (Prague: Calveské kněh-kupectwí, 1846), dedicated to 'the sons of my race in Bohemia'.

14 Sir Walter Scott, *Quentin Durward* (1823), here quoted from *The Prose Works of Sir Walter Scott*, vol. 3 (Paris: A. and W. Galignani, 1827), p. 745.

15 F. S. Chrismar, *Skizzen einer Reise durch Ungarn in die Türkei* (Pesth: Georg Kilian jun., 1834), especially the chapter 'Die Zigeuner', pp. 65–9.

16 On Mácha and Hegelianism, see Procházka, 'Byron in Czech Culture' (n. 2 above), pp. 293–6.

17 'Das Epos, indem es zum Gegenstande hat, was ist, erhält das Geschehen einer Handlung zum Objekte, die in ihrer ganzen Breite der Umstände und Verhältnisse als reiche Begebenheit im Zusammenhange mit der in sich totalen Welt einer Nation und Zeit zur Anschauung gelangen muß ... Als solch eine ursprüngliche Totalität ist das epische Werk die Sage, das Buch, die Bibel eines Volks, und jede große und bedeutende Nation hat dergleichen absolut erste Bücher, in denen ihr, was ihr ursprünglicher Geist ist, ausgesprochen wird': Hegel, *Vorlesungen über die Ästhetik*, part 3, *Abschnitt 3*, Chapter 3, III/A/1/c, 'Die eigentliche Epopöe', here quoted from H.G. Hotho, ed., *Georg Wilhelm Friedrich Hegel's Vorlesungen über die Aesthetik*, part 3 (= *Georg Wilhelm Friedrich Hegel's Werke: Vollständige Ausgabe*, vol. 10/3, 2nd ed., Berlin: Duncker und Humblot, 1843), pp. 331–2.

18 Grellmann, *Historischer Versuch* (n. 9 above, 2nd ed., 1787), pp. 167–8, quoting László Turóczi, who recounts the story already in the first edition of his *Ungaria suis cum regibus compendio data* (Trnava [Tyrnau]: Typis Academicis Soc. Jesu per Fridericum Gall, 1729), pp. 176–7. In fact there were several published versions of this legend before 1835, any of which could have served as Mácha's source; another is in Clemens Brentano, *Die mehreren Wehmüller und ungarischen Nationalgesichter* (1817), towards the end of the tale 'Das Pickenick des Katers Mores: Erzählung des kroatischen Edelmanns'.

19 Bartoloměj Daniel, 'Romská píseň v Máchových Cikánech' [The Roma Song in Mácha's *Gypsies*], *Česká literatura*, vol. 45 (1997), pp. 85–9.

20 Josef Kajetán Tyl, *Fidlovačka, aneb Žádný hněv a žádná rvačka: obrazy života pražského ve čtyřech odděleních [Fidlovačka, or No Anger and No Brawling: Images of Prague Life, in Four Acts]* (1834), published in Josef Kajetán Tyl, *Dramatické spisy* [Dramatic Works], vol. 3 (Prague: B. Kočí, 1906).

21 Franz Liszt [and others], *Des Bohémiens et de leur musique en Hongrie* (1st ed., Paris: Librairie Nouvelle – A. Bourdilliat, 1859; 2nd ed., Leipzig: Breitkopf & Härtel, 1881; first German translation, ed. Peter Cornelius, Pesth: G. Heckenast, 1861).

22 Nicholas Saul, *Gypsies and Orientalism in German Literature and Anthropology of the Long Nineteenth Century* (London: Legenda / Modern Humanities Research Association and Maney Publishing, 2007). Saul's account of Grellmann and of Liszt is essential reading.

BIBLIOGRAPHY

The secondary literature on Mácha, and on the Gypsies as a motif in nineteenth-century literature and nineteenth-century music, is very extensive, mainly in Czech; the selective listing here complements some of the items quoted in the Introduction with further material, in English, French, and German, which may be accessible and of interest to English-speaking readers.

Stefanie Bach, 'Musical Gypsies and Anti-Classical Aesthetics: The Romantic Reception of Goethe's Mignon Character in Brentano's *Die mehreren Wehmüller und ungarische Nationalgesichter*', *Music and Literature in German Romanticism*, ed. Siobhán Donovan and Robin Elliott (Woodbridge: Boydell & Brewer, 2004), pp. 105–22

Jonathan Bellman, *The Style Hongrois in the Music of Western Europe* (Boston, MA: Northeastern University Press, 1993)

Terence Cave, *Recognitions: A Study in Poetics* (Oxford, UK: Clarendon Press, 1988)

Peter Demetz, *Böhmen böhmisch: Essays* (Vienna: Paul Zsolnay, 2006)

Alfred French, ed., *Anthology of Czech Poetry* (Ann Arbor, MI: Czechoslovak Society for Arts and Sciences in America / Department of Slavic Languages and Literatures of the University of Michigan, 1973)

Henri Granjard, *Mácha et la Renaissance nationale en Bohême* (Paris: Institut d'Études slaves de l'Université de Paris, 1957)

Kamila Kinyon, '*Hynutí* in Karel Hynek Mácha's *Máj*: The Imperishability of Perishing', *European Romantic Review*, vol. 9 (1998), pp. 519–34

Franz Liszt [and others], *Des Bohémiens et de leur musique en Hongrie* (1st ed., Paris: Librairie Nouvelle – A. Bourdilliat, 1859; 2nd ed., Leipzig: Breitkopf et Haertel, 1881; first German translation, ed. Peter Cornelius, Pesth: G. Heckenast, 1861)

Shay Loya, *Liszt's Transcultural Modernism and the Hungarian-Gypsy Tradition* (Rochester, NY: University of Rochester Press, 2011)

Anna G. Piotrowska, trans. Guy R. Torr, *Gypsy Music in European Culture from the Late Eighteenth to the Early Twentieth Centuries* (Boston, MA: Northeastern University Press, 2013)

Martin Procházka, 'Byron in Czech Culture', *The Reception of Byron in Europe*, vol. 2 (*Northern, Central, and Eastern Europe*), ed. Richard A. Cardwell (London & New York: Thoemmes Continuum, 2004), pp. 283–304

Alexander Pushkin, trans. Antony Wood, *The Gypsies* [1827] *& Other Narrative Poems* (Boston, MA: David R. Godine, 2006)

Robert B. Pynsent, *Czech Prose and Verse: A Selection with an Introductory Essay* (London: Athlone Press, University of London, 1979), esp. pp. xxii–xxiii [still reflecting the older view questioning Mácha's authorship of *Gypsies*]

Robert B. Pynsent, 'Mácha, Karel Hynek', *The Everyman Companion to East European Literature*, ed. Robert B. Pynsent and S. I. Kanikova (London: Dent, 1993), p. 241

Nicholas Saul, *Gypsies and Orientalism in German Literature and Anthropology of the Long Nineteenth Century* (London: Legenda / Modern Humanities Research Association and Maney Publishing. 2007)

Efraim Sicher, *The Jew's Daughter: A Cultural History of a Conversion Narrative* (Lanham, MD: Lexington Books, 2017)

Wilhelm Solms and Daniel Strauss, eds., *Zigeunerbilder in der deutschsprachigen Literatur* (Heidelberg: Dokumentations- und Kulturzentrum deutscher Sinti und Roma, 1995)

Wilhelm Solms, *Zigeunerbilder: Ein dunkles Kapitel der deutschen Literaturgeschichte, von der frühen Neuzeit bis zur Romantik* (Würzburg: Königshausen & Neumann, 2008)

René Wellek, *Essays on Czech Literature* (The Hague: Mouton, 1963)

GYPSIES

BY KAREL HYNEK MÁCHA

1

Long my journey –
a vain quest! –

A tale is sometimes told in a far-off land,
like the cold rustle of a stream when it flows over cold lips,
that once upon a time, a young man appeared from far away.

STEFAN GARCZYŃSKI
The History of Wacław (1832)

Ah! he would be transported into bygone times,
better places, into a famous, distant land;
on the banks of the Jordan, beneath a palm tree,
musing, he would recline with his Hebrew kin.

Ah, no – the conflicts of former concerns are now ceased,
there remains only the quiet grave of vanished hope;
the light of joyfulness that once burned in her eyes
was extinguished – and with its smoke her whole face was darkened.

ANTONI MALCZEWSKI
Maria, A Ukrainian Romance (1825)

YOU SILENT LANDSCAPE! How often has your solitude enticed me into its shadows, so that calm might be restored to my raging heart! How often has your silence returned, that lodged in my soul, a peace lost to my senses? But now – to one grown grey in your overgrown rocks – you seem an abyss to

1

me; unleashing terrible imaginings in my restless mind, you revive hideous fables in my memory, and now you will never restore calm to my breast. – Once more I wander among your rocks; the pale moon has risen over the darkness of the black fir trees, and its lifeless eyes gaze silently into the face of a solitary man – and yet profound misery seizes my breast, and yet the profound tranquillity of times past will, alas, never return now. So in the tearstained morning a cold mist rests on the stony breast of your hillsides. And past times, lost like the beam of a distant star, sometimes penetrate merely the vision of my soul; clear is their light, but it gives no warmth.

In the midst of the fertile plain lies a valley, deep, narrow, but many miles in length. A traveller on the vast plain does not expect the dale lying before him; when all at once he comes to its edge and, appalled, checks his step, as if the earth had suddenly burst open before him, far beneath him he will spy the tops of dark firs, and, here and there among the rocks, of scattered cottages. High precipices loom over both sides of this valley, yet the two sides are very dissimilar.

Immediately on the left-hand side, there stands a high, steep, sandy ledge. Many a rain has abraded it into disparate forms of strange animals, and of defaced human figures, which, seething in an innumerable swarm, seem to climb the rock wall or to stare out from it, gazing at the traveller from their hollow eyes. Close to the ledge, along its outcrops and their crevices, tall firs and pines overshadow these often horrifying freaks of nature, in places affording the eye of the wayfarer an uninterrupted view of the yellowish-white rock wall, but only from below.

On the right-hand side, from the east plunging down to the west, the sandy rock is split apart in many boulders of irregular size, and, rising higher and higher after one another over the valley, these form, sporadically, an enormous, sprawling flight of stairs. Dense bushes grow from the great rocks towering over them, and the whole hillside resembles a desolate city of Oriental lands, over whose uniform roofs, overgrown with moss, yellowing birches bow their weeping branches; in whose streets thick undergrowth covers the narrow access into a deserted building that now serves only wary foxes as a shelter.

Here and there, some stone juts out, as if a slender turret were rising steeply over the flat roofs, and rain and other misfortunes have fashioned narrow windows so that the deception might be complete. Some cottages, if these six or seven huts may be called this, cling, fitfully, to these stones densely set on the hillside; and many of these huts have mere broken façades of unhewn timber, fronting caves within the stones. A narrow path leads from one hut to another among the crevices of the rocks, through the dense undergrowth, down into the valley, to a narrow lake, long and deep, upon whose bluish surface water-lilies extend their broad, dark green leaves, and their pale blossoms drift like silver coronets above the dark mirror of the waters. If, as many scholars aver, the entire Czech land was simply a single great lake in the most ancient times, then this is a tiny remnant of those immense waters, and its narrow, flat banks on either side are great steps in the sandy rock that extends into the watery depths, who knows how far; for, as far as the local inhabitants know, no one has ever plumbed the depths of these waters.

By the lake, at the outflow of a small stream, stands a tiny mill, whose monotonous knocking, combined with the rustling and whistling of the birds flying by, makes this wilderness seem yet more desolate, makes the oppression of this landscape seem yet more terrible. At last, the melody of a folk-song, uttered by an invisible shepherd, shyly steals in, and, as if charmed by it, the landscape repeats his song several times to itself in a dark – then darker – echo.

About six hundred paces from the outflow, where the little stream, shaded by dense clumps of alders, chatters more volubly to its native landscape in a little waterfall, the valley breaks open on the left-hand side into a second dale, broader, but short. In the middle of this stands a high rock, densely overgrown, crowned with the ruins of an old castle; but the rocky walls of this valley encircling it are much higher, and even the single high tower of the ruined castle does not rise higher than the peaks of the firs on the hill bordering these immense walls.

The castle building, especially in its round towers, is wholly gauged to replicate the quiet horror of the landscape. Pale yellow, like the rock, its base seems to consist of a single piece. Its wall is of enormous thickness, and it has not a single window, right up to the pointed stone roof, which is also yellowed. It is completely uniform and smooth, and the minor adornments set under its protection, like a giant's necklace, make its horrific force weigh all the more terrifyingly on the astonished, erring pilgrim. In a somewhat broader shelter there trembles a young birch tree, adjacent to the low pointed roof, and drooping from it towards the valley, like the single feather in a robber's hat.

Under this castle, at the entrance to this second dale, stands a little cottage, close above the stream, of the unexceptional, humble construction that is common there. Like the other huts on the second hill, it too is supported at the rear by a rock, and differs from them only in that its front section, extended along it, is covered by a grapevine with its broad leaves. In front of it is a small rectangular garden, in which two stone tables, raised on the turf, surrounded by turf seats, as well as a garland dangling above the doors, proclaim this cottage to be the only inn in this landscape.

One evening, the shepherds guiding their flocks home between the low bushes on the opposite hill saw three persons indistinctly in this little garden, and on that same evening begins the tale that I heard told in that same garden.

As the shepherds quickly guessed, it was the occupant of this cottage, his daughter, and their regular daily visitor, who were the three persons in the 'little Jewish garden', as the neighbours called it.

The first person was an old man, tall, aged seventy, a faithful son of the Israelite race. Stooping a little, he sauntered at a leisurely pace through the little garden, from one end to the other. His black velvet trousers, reaching to his knees, with their silver buckles, his matching waistcoat with its large silver buttons, and the silver buckles on his gleaming shoes, bore witness that poverty was not the master here as it was in the other cottages. Likewise, his clean white stockings, the white sleeves of his fine shirt, and the white collar at his throat, did not betoken a cleanliness unusual in his nation, but rather the fact that it was the Sabbath – for on other days his supple though aging figure was hidden under a reddish coat, both tattered and filthy. Only his long white beard, combed for the day, and reaching down to his waist, revealed his ripe old age, and a small black velvet hat covered his head, for his thin strands of grey hair were incapable of protecting it from the evening breeze. At other times, he moved around, nimble and avaricious, either serving or sitting at table with his guests; but today he walked with his solemn face at times turned heavenward, and at times to the ground, and from his movements it could be deduced that he was reciting his customary prayers.

In a porch in front of the cottage sat his daughter, Leah, a tall, slender figure, in eccentric rather than practical dress. Her pleated white robe, ankle-length over her bare feet, was secured with a black belt shot through with silver. Her head was wrapped in a high Turkish turban, in the manner of the womenfolk of her nation who live in Oriental lands, and thick black locks cascaded around her beautiful, pale face, below this headdress, on to her white neck. Her great dark eyes, staring into the infinite distance, glittered brightly; however, her fixed gaze into the blue void, and the strange expression on her face, together with her attire, made it easy to conjecture that she was not normal. Her hands played listlessly with a flower, tearing off its petals.

The third person, a daily guest in this little inn, was an old veteran, renowned in these parts as a supreme storyteller. Whenever a blue coat with red epaulettes gleamed in the valley, it was certainly this man, and the children would rush out of the cottages to meet him, begging him to tell them a story. He never disappointed them, either, but, twirling his impressive moustache, and seating himself on the ground among them, would tell them long stories, even when urgent work was to be done.

Besides this, he enjoyed another, more profitable, office, at the castle, close to the entrance to the valley already described. There he was obliged to provide the lord and the officials with clean apparel every day; for this service, and because he had earlier served his lord in battle as his batman, he enjoyed free accommodation in the castle, and a monthly allowance in addition. However, this money was never enough; for as soon as he received it at the end of the month, he was immediately obliged to use it to repay his debts to the old Jew, whom he patronized every day for the sake of his tipples. Previously he had also been a castle messenger; however, inasmuch as no one could ever expect him to come back, after he had been sent out, if children encountered him and asked for a story, he was dismissed as messenger, and his salary was reduced, according to his own scale of measurement, by a few glasses. Certainly, he would not have sat by himself on a turf seat at a stone table if the children had not been kept at home so late in the evening, by strict order of their parents, and by their terror of the monsters that roamed the valley at night, if the stories he told were true.

Because no one here was listening to him, he was repeating the whole story of the Napoleonic wars to himself, and, as was his habit, very loudly, in such a way that every few words were capped by a bald fabrication, which was immediately transparent to everyone. Lies had become his inveterate habit, so that failing anyone else he was obliged to lie to himself. Intermittently he would nod and wave, as if he were exceedingly surprised by all he said, and sometimes, breaking off in the midst of the narrative, he would swill out his throat with his liquor, and disjointed 'Aye, aye!' interjections would glide out of his mouth, swathed with its luxuriant moustache. Meanwhile, he was constantly scanning the valley, which was visible at a great distance from here.

The sun had long set, and isolated red streaks flickered over the new moon, which hung just over the old tower, like a silver lamp in a hall of clouds. In its light, a pale birch tree on the tower fluttered its new leaves, like dead embers, over the pallid ruins. Terrifying figures seemed to be intermingling on the rock wall in the twinkling light, and a silent moonbeam rested above the rocky ledge on the opposite side, like desolate oblivion over a deserted city, playing in the birch trees of its gravestones. The thick bushes in the deserted streets swayed back and forth as if in a light breeze, whispering like the fading voice of a muezzin calling from the minarets to the prayers of the orthodox departed, and the slender stones towering like turrets over the ruins of an Oriental city gleamed like silver domes in the pale radiance. Sparks seemed to be flying over the stream; but the silent image of the moon was floating in the mirror of the surface of the lake, among the water-lilies and the stars of heaven. The surrounding hills, and the darker trees, took on their colours, and only their tops turned red here and there in the glow of the dying fires.

The herdsmen on the horizon drove their flocks across over the hills into their quiet stalls; their melodies were silenced, together with the knocking of the little mill, and in the deep quiet, nothing was to be heard except the bubbling of the stream and the veteran's noisy conversation with himself about the Napoleonic wars.

'On the left, there was a high mountain – about here,' he said, putting his hat into the place in question, with his left hand. 'On the right, the church tower of some village poked out of a copse of trees – about hereabouts,' and taking his glass, he put it on the right, to represent the tower in question; then, jabbing with his thumb, in the middle of the table, he continued: 'And here we were standing – or – no, no – we weren't standing, that would be a lie; – here we were sitting – yes, I was, at any rate – and I was sitting right on the bass drum, opposite the French. Aye, aye! – What? You don't believe it? On my word, who would dare – now, now, just so, we were sitting here, and we remained seated, but not for long, – for all of a sudden, there's a bang behind me on that bass drum, right behind me, and – and – and,' meanwhile caressing the stone table with outstretched hand, but suddenly yelling very abruptly: 'and the whole army jumped out – be damned – pooh – the whole army! Ha, ha! What? Who would dare? Now, now, the whole army, and even if it wasn't the whole army, I swear, I jumped out – yes, so I did – and I spin round, and behind me there's the general himself standing – upon my word, by himself, and all the officers behind him. – And here he taps me on the shoulder, no – no, that'd be a lie; here he grabs me by my button – yes, on my word, by my button!' At that, he banged the tower, or glass, on the table, drained it, and made it clatter on the table as loudly as if all three bells were ringing in the tower.

Immediately, the serving girl ran out of the cottage, and, curtseying to the elderly Jew, took the glass from the hand of the veteran. The latter, however, grasping her hand, and saying: 'Yes, look, by my button, by this very one, or no – no – that'd be a lie,' began to continue his story. However, the girl, used to such behaviour, and pulling herself away, with the glass, ran into the cottage, and the veteran Bárta, or Bárta Flacon, as the neighbours called him, pressed on with his lies: 'And here he says to me, "Bárta, do you see that tower over there?" I say, "Yes, I see it!" Now, now – where's that tower gone? – Aha!' At that, the girl brought a full glass, and, placing it next to the hat, again disappeared. 'Oho!' cried Bárta, 'it wasn't here – just here, right here,' and, moving the glass to the left of the hat, on the other side of the table, went on speaking: 'And, to finish the story, here I am, I went with this chap to spy out that village, and we went and we drank – we drank till the hills turned green. – I'd had three – four pints, and he'd had just one, – but after that – afterwards he began to drink, and after I'd had my fifth, here he'd drunk – and – and,' and again he caressed the table with his hand, a gesture that always presaged excessive lies, until, after a pause, he abruptly shouted: 'Be damned! He'd drunk four barrels – pooh – be damned! Aye, aye, so it was! Four barrels! On my word, four barrels! And after that we went spying. He – and I. He was in front and I went behind, and I was hiding so smartly behind those four barrels, that I couldn't see anything in front of me – not a damned thing.' – Used to his listeners laughing during the telling of this story, which was a regular occurrence, he laughed noisily himself. 'Ha, ha, ha! – What? Who would dare? Now – now – ten soldiers came out upon us – and – one of them says: "Who goes there?" – And that chap who was with

me shouts out and says, "We're spies!" and gives him a whack –
and – and,' dragging his hand over the table, he yelled, 'and all
forty fell! – Aye, aye! – Yes! Be damned! All forty! Aye! – And
that tower – ' At that, he raised the glass, and took a draught as
heartily as if he were wanting to drain all four barrels at once. –

Over the now silent landscape, all at once there began to be
heard some resonant string chords – they were carried across the
quiet valley, and, echoed from the rocks, they melted away into
dark, enchanting music. – Then there was silence once more.

2

An exile!...
Yearning encompasses me, disquiets oppress me,
Everything I see is not mine!
Heaven, earth, air, people and speech,
each is yearning, even when new.

JULIAN URSYN NIEMCEWICZ
Lamentations of an Exile (1833)

AFTER A TIME, a few mournful sounds were to be heard from the opposite hill. Bárta, open-mouthed, and with glass in hand, quickly stared up at the opposite hill and also at the old castle; even the old Jew stood still and listened in astonishment. Leah alone remained immobile as she had been at first. Immediately after this, a song followed. The veteran Bárta rose hurriedly, and placing his hat aslant on his head, took up a military posture and stared motionlessly. The mournful song was precisely enunciated, every word was clear, and sorrowful string music filled the short pauses between the stanzas:

> *Breezes rustle in the ample wheatfield,*
> *blossoms deck the rose-white apple tree,*
> *golden ears of harvest bow before me,*
> *all inclining – yet not greeting me.*

Breezes softly play across the birch wood,
ancient oak tree watches, strong and free,
oak leaves whisper hidden, buried secrets;
all I hear – yet not a word for me.

Silver voices bubble in the furrow,
stream embraces blossoms in the lea,
telling tales of long departed heroes;
though I listen – nothing speaks to me.

Azure vault of heaven soars above me,
clouds impelled by breezes go and come,
north today – tomorrow driven southward,
westward – eastward – never towards my home.

Scattered is my nation; and my brethren
strangers each to each; in tears I burn,
nowhere resting, ever tramping onwards,
ever farther, never to return.

At the words 'scattered is my nation', Leah rose abruptly; after passing her pale hand over her face, she listened attentively with unblinking eyes staring into the remote distance, until the end of the song. When the strings and their echo had died away, and the deep silence all around returned, a mournful song of her own resounded in the deep valley.

Jerusalem desolate, mourning in bitterness,
scattered my nation, abhorred in the earth,
no stone for a pillow, no place for a refuge,
her fathers' graves lost in the land of her birth.

13

From paradise banished – O palms at the Jordan,
hearing at sunrise the voice of the dove,
greet there my distant land, far from my vision,
tell her I cherish for ever her love.

That love my companion, across a high mountain,
more high than that mountain o'er which I must part;
we sailed over ocean – across the deep ocean;
more deep than that ocean – the grief in my heart.

The old Jew stood there in silence; tears flowed over his weathered face and over his grey beard. For some time he stood thus. – Bárta clasped his hands in amazement, and a murmured 'aye, aye' from his mouth accompanied Leah's song. During this song, two tall figures made their way on the other side of the hill along the footpath among the rocks, from cottage to cottage, down into the valley. – Leah's song fell silent, and its last echoes died away over the rocks of the opposite side, as if they had drifted off to sleep in the ray of the setting moon over a desolate Jerusalem.

The old veteran, as if awoken from slumber, and roused by the final words of the song, began babbling once more: 'I've been to sea as well – yes – to sea – we were there for three days – oh, it's strange at sea – you don't see anything except water and sky – on my word! – And all that roaring from the cannons there at sea! – Well, a hundred times louder! – no, no, that'd be a lie – well, five times at least – yes, assuredly five times!'

Who knows what he would have gone on to say, and for how long, if the newcomers had not interrupted him. They were two Gypsies. In front came a short youth, in Hungarian attire: he was clothed in red trousers embroidered in gold, yellow shoes, and a tight blue jacket adorned with gold braid. His head was bare, but his long, thick, black hair sufficed to protect his head from the vagaries of the weather. His figure was slim and slight, and his head, like his whole person, was bent to the right. His right hand was noticeably larger than his left, and out of habit he kept his eyes constantly turned to the ground; but his face was handsome, with an especially high, proudly arched forehead, and a dark blue eye, whose intermittent desolate intensity elicited involuntary sympathy. The second Gypsy, much older, was dressed entirely in blue, and less extravagantly. – His dark eyes, above sunburnt cheeks, blazed like twin stars in the evening sky. The younger one had a dulcimer slung over his shoulder, with glittering strings; the older one carried under his arm a musical instrument resembling our violin. They were wandering musicians.

The young Gypsy moved forward, but, nonplussed, seeing the veteran and the others, withdrew a couple of paces, as if he had been expecting someone else. Recovering his composure, however, he asked whether there was an inn here. 'Oh, absolutely; come in, sirs – come in – here you can get pleasantly drunk – I know it well – on my word! Just come in!' – With this welcome, Bárta clinked his glass on the table, and the girl ran out of the cottage. The old Jew, who had meanwhile resumed walking in the garden, intermittently pausing by the porch and sadly gazing at his daughter, hurriedly came across to the newcomers, and inquired after their wishes affably – or rather, unctuously – meanwhile murmuring disjointed words of the prayers from which he had been interrupted by the tinkling of the glass. Bárta, meanwhile, gave directions to the girl: 'Quick! get on with it! these gentlemen are on a journey, and that makes people hungry, on my word!'

Meanwhile, the young Gypsy, taking the musical instrument from his shoulder, asked her to bring bread and water; and the girl, running into the cottage, quickly returned with the bread and water. The old Jew now again walked the garden in prayer, ignoring the wayfarers, whether because he thought that they were not very talkative, or because he suspected that he was not likely to gain much trade from them.

Bárta shook his head in surprise: 'Bread and water? On my word! aye, aye! on my word! That time on the Rhine, things were different then. We came to this cottage – and were we hungry! on my word! So hungry I could have eaten an elephant! Aye, aye – and do you think I've never eaten elephant? – On my word, excellent meat, and elephant soup's even better! Aye, aye – what – don't you believe me? – Who would dare? – Now – now where was I stopping? – Aha, in that cottage! Or – no – no – that'd be a lie – I didn't stop there – no, because I came out of it. There was an old grandmamma sitting in the cottage, blind, deaf, and smoking tobacco – aye, aye – yes, smoking, on my word! Every living creature smokes there – everything – I saw with my own eyes there, or no – no, I heard, that in those parts,' now, speaking more ponderously, and scraping his hand over the table, 'yes, that in those parts – be damned!' – and now very fast – 'even the pigs smoke! Be damned! – Pooh – ha, ha, ha! What? Who would dare? – Now – now – where was I stopping, yes – in front of that cottage, or no – no, that'd be a lie, I didn't

16

stop there, but we went on; that's two of us, soldiers, Bartoloměj Bárta, that's me, and Franta, the potter's son. – He was
still alive then, and he was in the army, yes, there with me. They
killed him among the parley-voos at what-d'ye-call-it – what's
its name, it's on the tip of my tongue, it's just over the Rhine –
yes, at what-d'ye-call-it! – So then, when he was still alive, he
was just as hungry as I was, and we went into the village to
see where we could catch something. And here we go, and we
go past a hole, and something is screeching in it. Yes – on my
word – past a hole – it was as big as my hat! or no – no, that'd be
a lie, about as big as this one in my sleeve – yes! We're listening
to find out what's screeching – the hole led into some sort of
pigsty, down on the ground, and we couldn't make out what
was screeching; is it a cock or a hen? And Franta's there in front
and I'm against the wall. Franta calls out, I unsheathe my sword
and I keep watch – yes, keep watch; on my word; I keep quiet,
I don't even breathe. – And here it sticks out its head, a head as
big – well, as my hat – aye, aye – ' he drank, and after a pause
continued, 'on my word – a horn on each end – on my word,
aye, aye – I shuddered, but I pull myself together, I strike, and in
one stroke I've cut it off. Aye, aye! – On my word, in one stroke,
look here – with this sabre!' With that he flung his sabre on to
the stone table. 'Yes, in one stroke! And what had I cut off?' –

Up to this point, the Gypsies had been sitting quietly,
ignoring the veteran. The old Gypsy, sitting directly opposite
him, was buried in deep thought; now and again, he clenched
his fist impulsively in the air in front of him, and his eye was
meanwhile darting hither and thither. All his behaviour beto-
kened immense restlessness. The younger Gypsy was gazing

17

around over the landscape, and, sighing deeply, he was uttering disjointed words in an incomprehensible language. With the clatter of the sabre on the table, as if awoken from dreams, they turned their attention to the veteran, who stood in front of them, clutching the table, and pointing with out-stretched hand at the sabre: 'Aye, aye – yes – yes – Franta grabbed it and we went home – and –'

The older Gypsy rose and went off along the footpath into the valley, and could be seen after a time in the gloom among the rocks and bushes, creeping into the old castle. Above, there was still flickering light in the moon's ray, which, fading behind the tops of the highest firs, still illuminated the pale ruins and the high tower, whose faint shadow stretched far over the opposite side.

The young Gypsy, turning to the veteran, asked him, however, whether he was often a patron there.

'Me?' he replied, 'me? Every day. It's clear that you –'

The Gypsy went on, 'Are you well-known in this place?' 'I – I –' replied the veteran, 'Oh, I know every nook and cranny! I –'

'Have you lived here long?'

'I – we came here with his lordship from the wars, from the Rhineland – aye – aye, yes –'

'Was that long ago?'

'Yes indeed, don't you know? It's been ten – fifteen – sixteen – seventeen years – yes – on my word! – seventeen years.'

'I have also been here once, I don't know how long ago,' said the Gypsy. 'I came to Prague this way with my father, and we stayed overnight in the inn here. At that time there was someone else managing the inn, a woman.'

'That's a long time ago now, yes, about fifteen – sixteen years, it could be – aye – on my word – you must have been little – yes – on my word, very little!'

'I was about four years old, travelling with my father,' replied the Gypsy. 'And do you know,' he asked, 'what has happened to that landlady?'

'Yes – that was a strange woman – strange –,' said the veteran, pleased that he had found someone who would listen to his stories. And now he began his narration, frequently interjecting 'aye, aye', and making noisy fun of himself from time to time.

He was already soundly drunk, and during the narration he went on drinking even more soundly, so that it seemed that today he would never reach the end of his story. 'Yes, a strange woman – on my word – and why – I know very well. – She was strange, and came here, no one knows where from – no one – I didn't know either, – because she had arrived here before I came. But I remember it well, very well, – when we arrived with his lordship from the Rhine, evening had fallen, it was pouring with rain, and it was pitch dark. I had a white coat on and I was on horseback, very downcast. – We were riding in the forest, and according to his lordship we were half an hour from the castle, to which we'd sent word in advance that we were coming. There in the forest a female form was standing under a great oak tree, under the old oak there by the charnel stone, as we say – in the pouring rain. And as we're trotting – no, no – that'd be a lie, we didn't trot – we were walking, yes, walking – his lordship in front, me behind him – And now that woman leaps out at us –' (scraping his hand across the table and speaking in a low voice – and then suddenly shouting loudly) 'be damned! twenty-five foot tall – yes - pooh, twenty-five foot, right in front of us – aye, aye!' Meanwhile, he took his glass, and took a long draught, as if wishing to give the Gypsy time to marvel at this. 'On my word,' continued Bárta, 'twenty-five foot, – and her eyes gleamed – like a pair of torches. Then taking his lordship's horse, she cries, "Now he's here, now you're here!" with a great shout. His lordship, scared, gets the horse away with his spurs, I did too – and away we flew – white coats flying behind us through that rain, out of the forest, and she was rolling in the mud – no – no, that'd be a lie, not in the mud, but in the wet sand, because there's nothing but sand in the forest under the charnel stone.' – Listening attentively, the Gypsy rose quickly at these words, and pressed his clenched fist against the stone table; his teeth could be heard grinding loudly. Passing his smaller left hand over his face, however, he seated himself again, and it seemed that he was at ease, listening to the veteran, who went on: 'And we're racing for a quarter of an hour, and here' – again scraping his hand along the table, then shouting very quickly – 'be damned, here's that woman racing up to us – I don't know which way she'd taken to get there, and which way we took I don't know either; but it seemed to me that we were once again at that place, at the charnel stone – again under the old oak, – and she's standing there, and she's raising her hands, and she's turning white, and her eyes are blazing, and she's screaming; we take to our heels all the more, and we fly, and we arrived at the castle late at night, which way – I don't know. That was the first time I'd been there – yes, the first time. His lordship took me out of the army with him from the Rhine, so I didn't know anything.'

At that, the Gypsy made a slight gesture, as if wishing to ask a question; Bárta, however, would not be deflected from his story, and quickly continued: 'His lordship wouldn't say a word the whole evening, aye, aye – yes, not even a whisper, and first of all he told me to go to the devil – it looked to me as if he was weeping. And me, I went to the devil, and I went, and I asked, and I got as far as the inn. There comes the landlady – and it's the same woman who had been in the forest, on my word, the same one – and she had a little boy with her, about four years old. – I'm terrified of her, and that boy – he was just like you, bent towards the right, and stooping forwards, yes, and his eyes were flashing just as yours do now; yes – and I'm terrified, I jump up and run away – she's after me, and I've no idea how I got back to the castle that night. In the morning she had to leave the village; his lordship commanded it, and sent her word by me that she had to leave, that he was not to set eyes on her little boy again, and something or other else; – a day later – the little boy was gone – and no one knows where he had gone – aye – aye.' He drank some more, giving the Gypsy time to register his astonishment, but the latter, sinking his head in his hands, gave a deep sigh.

'For several nights after that,' continued Bárta, 'she wandered around the castle, until his lordship finally let her in; – I don't know why, I don't know what for, I don't know, and I don't know anything; but I well remember, all of it, as if it were yesterday – yes – as if it were yesterday! And there she used to be, she and his lordship, they were often together;

I used to see it. And all kinds of womenfolk used to come to us with her; I don't know where from. Everyone thought no one knew anything, but me – I – be damned, I was upon the lookout for it all. I used to wonder what it was for – and where that landlady had been before that – and no one knew anything, except that it was eleven – no, twenty-six – twenty-seven – twenty-eight years ago – yes, twenty-eight, that she came to the castle, just when his lordship came back from Italy, and no one knew where she had come from, and that his lordship granted her the inn here. After that, it used to be said, his lordship used to go to her, and they called her Angelina – yes, on my word, Angelina. Afterwards, on the very same day, her ladyship is supposed to have borne a son, now that's about twenty-two years ago – yes, twenty-two years –, that son of hers is supposed to have had a birthmark on his breast, which is supposed to have been like a bloodstained hand, and she is supposed to have been very ill then, – very ill. Both her ladyship and her ladyship's son are supposed to have died immediately, though – two hours later – yes, two hours. But they said that his lordship went off straight away to the army, and he came back with me four years later. That's all – yes, that's all.'

The young Gypsy, captivated, listened closely to the whole story, sighing deeply from time to time; but not a single word disclosed what the reason might be for his grief. Impetuously, he now asked: 'Where would that former landlady be now?'

'Where is she now?' replied Bárta. 'The devil only knows. Her residence in the castle, which I told you about before, continued for almost nine – ten years – yes, ten years. Towards

22

the end that devil did get me, and I went to the inn here, to the Jew who got the cottage here after her. But I used to see all kinds of womenfolk coming and going when I went home at night – yes – and his lordship used to be very merry. Afterwards I saw the former landlady very seldom; that Angelina was supposed to be very strange – yes – very strange. Up to about seven or eight years ago, they had locked her up in the castle tower – and she escaped – no one knows where she went. The last one to see her on the day she escaped was Honza Loučkovic, at the old oak by the charnel stone, and from that day to this no one has heard anything about her. She'd gone – that one, – on my word!'

The Gypsy sat, immobile, in deep thought, staring before him into the nocturnal gloom; grief-stricken sighs and incomprehensible words fell by turns from his lips. The old Jew walked the garden in incessant prayer, stopping from time to time near Leah, who sat motionless, as she had before her answering song, ignoring all that was going on around her.

Bárta, having finished, took a long draught, and having drunk, clinked his glass on the table, repeating disjointed words under his breath, as if trying to establish whether he had forgotten anything: 'yes – seventeen years – charnel stone – little boy'. The girl came out of the cottage, but, instead of refilling his glass, told Bárta that it was nearly ten o'clock, while he, continuously clinking his glass on the table, went on: 'her ladyship – landlady'.

At this point, a little bell rang over the valley; its ring resounded from rock to rock, its answering echo lingering long in the distance – then there was silence.

'Excuse me, sir! – I must go now, yes, go. They ring at the castle here, and then everyone must return home to the castle. When they ring the second time, it'll be half past ten; and then they lock the castle, and whoever isn't in, won't be allowed in; for they don't open to anyone later than that – not to anyone, even me – ha, ha, ha! Now then, good night, good night – girl, make up a bed for this gentleman; look here – after a journey like this,' said Bárta, staggering out of the garden, 'after a journey like this, anyone would want to get some sleep; I tell you – on my word – I know it only too well.' At that, he was already below the garden in the valley, and only his muttering could be heard. Intermittently, in his talk, the words 'on the Rhine' emerged more loudly, 'yes – on my word – on the Rhine!', until, stumbling over the stream, he could no longer be seen or heard; and over the nocturnal landscape there descended a deep silence.

3

Covered in earth there, so many hundred bodies, names...

ADAM MICKIEWICZ
Ordon's Redoubt (1832)

As a beam o'er the face of the waters may glow
while the tide runs in darkness and coldness below,
so the cheek may be tinged with a warm sunny smile,
though the cold heart to ruin runs darkly the while.

THOMAS MOORE
Irish Melodies (1807)

Though wit may flash from fluent lips, and mirth distract the breast,
through midnight hours that yield no more their former hope of rest;
'tis but as ivy-leaves around the ruined turret wreath,
all green and wildly fresh without, but worn and grey beneath.

GEORGE GORDON, LORD BYRON
Stanzas for Music: There's Not a Joy the World can Give (1815)

THE MOON had now set, and a gloomy darkness stole across
the landscape. – The rocks and trees loomed in the inky black-
ness, and the dark tower of the ruined castle soared high in
the starry realm. In the cottages up the opposite hill, fires
glowed, and their light extended down into the dark valley

25

through the tiny windows. Pealing bells could be heard from the surrounding villages and the nearby small town, at ten o'clock every Saturday heralding the approaching celebration. – An indistinct figure was crawling in the nocturnal darkness out of the ruined castle. At times it was standing on a rocky outcrop, at times dropping down into the undergrowth. Now it stood in the narrow gate of the lower wall of the entrance; descending, it disappeared in the bushes, and only the clatter of a falling stone betrayed the crawling figure. It was the older Gypsy, returning from the derelict ruins.

The younger Gypsy sat, lost in thought, covering his sunburnt face with his hands. 'Alone, alone, then? – yet nothing? – gone? – unknown – no homeland?' and other strange words flowed disjointedly from his half-closed lips. The old Gypsy walked at an unconstrained pace along the footpath from the valley; coming into the garden, he sat down at the stone table without saying a word. 'No homeland – none – unknown native country!' continued the younger man. Raising his dulcimer, and striking its sonorous strings, he began to play a melody of deep mourning. After a time, the old Gypsy also picked up his musical instrument, and continued to play the melody to the accompaniment of the dulcimer. The melody was one of deep lamentation; as if in intimate grief, the tender strings of the dulcimer keened in a sorrowful song, and like loud weeping of distant sounds, the music radiated through the beautiful valley – through the gloomy night.

As the music progressed, the young Gypsy began to give the song a performance, not singing, but merely, as it were, narrating the tale; now in a high, now in a low voice, speeding

up or slowing down, as the scale of the music required. – It
was the Nagy-Iday song.[1]

Stag leaps free across the meadows,
hind in deepest forest wanders,
he upon a verdant carpet,
she beneath a verdant curtain;
he today, and she tomorrow
will chance on scattered race of Gypsies.

---

1   The Imperial Diet of 1556 condemned many Hungarian nobles as rebels;
    Wolfgang Buchheim and Marcel Dietrich were obliged to execute the verdict
    pronounced over them, for which they obtained 8,000 infantry, 600 heavy
    cavalry and the same number of hussars. After conquering the Tarkő castles
    of Újvár and Tarkő, they advanced on Perényi's fortress of Nagy-Ida. All the
    defenders of the besieged stronghold were Gypsies, who had been promised
    that if in defending their lord they held the stronghold, the whole district of
    their tribe would be given them as their own.
       For this undertaking, the Gypsies defended the stronghold so bravely
    that the assailants, disheartened by their many ineffective attacks, resolved
    to retreat. They had barely retreated, however, when the Gypsies rushed
    out of the fortress, impelled by premature joy, mocking the retreating forces,
    and declaring that if they had held out only a few more days at the fortress,
    their own lack of sufficient gunpowder and victuals would have forced
    them to surrender. This imprudent behaviour was reported to the retreating
    army. Immediately they turned around, stormed and conquered the fortress,
    and all the Gypsies were slaughtered by the enraged army, in return for
    their reckless boastfulness and their baseless derision. The memory of this
    bloodletting, which cost the lives of more than 1,000 people, remains alive
    to this day among the Gypsies, in a mournful, sorrowful melody, called
    the 'Nagy-Iday nóta'. – Every Gypsy knows this song, and if he hears it, his
    tears flow, he weeps, and he finally falls into loud groaning and despair.–
    I am unsure whether this is on account of the memory of the death of his
    brethren, or of the loss of his promised fatherland. For, although the Gypsy
    is weaned from his itinerant life only with difficulty, and seldom settles in
    one place, some obscure longing for an unknown homeland remains alive
    in him. [Mácha's footnote.]

Ravening bird above them circles,
in the rosy light of dawning;
eagle grey, high in the azure,
circling high above them, calling:

'Whence your grieving, Gypsy nation,
nation mine, O you my kinsfolk?
Grieving more than mists of morning?
Your abode, is it not beauteous? –
Azure dome its canopy.
Verdant mountains are its ramparts; –
moon and stars its radiant lanterns;
rosy dawn and rosy sunset
are its sumptuous purple hangings,
edged with boughs of summer blossoms,
hung before dark mountain walls.
Whence your grieving, Gypsy nation,
nation mine, O you my kinsfolk?'

The grieving nation gives him answer,
answers, with the stream lamenting:

'Ah, should we not make our moan?
Every beast his den has known,
yet Gypsies have no place to hide!
Every place where Gypsies stay
gives them rest for but one day,
then onwards, in the world so wide.

'Ah, should we not make our moan?
Every beast his prey has known,

yet Gypsies have no bread on earth!
Every man his land has earned,
to us no man has yet returned
what was stolen at our birth!

'Ah, should we not make our moan?
Endless roaming, endless woe,
no loving native land to know,
naught to melt our heart of stone?'

Lord of Nagy-Ida gives answer,
tethered lion, roars in answer:

'Shelter – homeland – I will grant you!
See how foes assail my country!
Be my shield, and guard this fortress,
be my defence – and in return,
castle, lands, all shall be yours;
here a homeland you shall find!'

Gypsies rise with strength of lions,
save the fortress – but their boasting
leads to Gypsies' full undoing.
Ah, the wolves turn on the stronghold,
turning, now devour the nation,
conquer the unhappy nation,
slaughter them with sword and halberd,
storm the fortress, promised birthright,
peaceful realm, their promised homeland!

Gypsy tribe, from homeland driven,
banished, – to a beauteous dwelling! –

Azure dome its canopy; –
verdant mountains are its ramparts; –
moon and stars its radiant lanterns.
Rosy dawn and rosy sunset
are its sumptuous purple hangings,
edged with boughs of summer blossoms,
hung before high mountain walls.

Whence your grieving, Gypsy nation,
nation mine, O you my kinsfolk? –

The voice of the narrator fell silent, and the music, repeating the melody of the final question, and reflected in a dark echo from the distant rocks, resounded in the valley like a faraway lament. During the song, the girl brought a lighted candle out of the cottage, and after placing it on the stone table, again disappeared. Although the older of the Gypsies immediately extinguished it, it was impossible for Leah, who, drawn by some mysterious yearning, had approached as soon as the song had started, not to notice the handsome face of the young Gypsy, with the expression of deep sorrow in his dark eyes, or to see the manifest tears on the unyielding, almost macabre, face of the older one. The old Jew also came near, drawn partly by the music and partly by his astonishment at his daughter.

After the conclusion of the song, Leah, loudly weeping, flung her arms around the neck of the young Gypsy, and her warm tears flowed on to his face. Long, long she wept; he embraced her tightly and drew her to his wildly beating heart, and their black hair, mingling in the dark night, merged in a dense veil around their faces. – Astonished, the older Gypsy gazed at them, and the old Jew, with clasped hands, with his face turned heavenwards, and his eyes raised to the starry sky, stood before them; on his face too there flowed tears, but tears of joy. After her copious weeping, Leah fell senseless at the feet of the Gypsy; the old Jew lifted up his daughter and took her into their silent dwelling. The Gypsies remained alone.

'Let us leave,' said the younger one. Immediately, the other rose, and eagerly moving towards the gate, said: 'Willingly! Onwards, on into the wide world! The dark night is my faithful friend.' – 'This is no place for us to remain,' said the young Gypsy, 'nor do I think it prudent; but I know other quarters, not far distant from here, where formerly only wild beasts used to take shelter.' Having paid the girl, who had emerged from the cottage, they left the garden by the footpath, around the low fence, leading down into the valley. Close to the mill, they crossed the stream by a small footbridge, and before long they were on the path uphill on the other side.

By the path, near the first cottage, the first level of the sandy rock was overgrown with dense bushes. Above the bushes there was a deep, dark cavity in this rock; cautiously, the young Gypsy crawled into this cavity, the old Gypsy meekly follow-ing, and both of them disappeared in the dark opening. On the further side of this rock, they crawled out again under the dense bushes out of the parted earth, and then crawled forward between the rocks, through narrow crevices and under the thick branches of the new growth of the bushes. It was pitch dark, and the dense bush merging from each rock to the next above them did not admit even a single ray of starlight on to their overgrown pathway. The young Gypsy, however, seemed very comfortably at home here. The older one followed close behind. Several times they squeezed through the narrowest of fissures, where they were able to make a way through only in single file; they had crawled over many a sandy rock, and now they were standing on a rather more open space in front of a high rock face. Now they crawled up a fissure in this rock, hidden by thick bushes; above, they crawled out over some stone levels, through a narrow hole, under the open sky, and stood high above the valley on the extensive rocks. Deep below them lay the beautiful dale – the lake – the Jews' cottage – the ruined castle – and far, far into the distance stretched the rocky walls, until the eye could perceive nothing in the distance but dark shadows on the horizon of the starry heavens. In the middle of the rock surface on which they were standing was an extensive oak thicket. Approaching this, the young Gypsy parted its branches, and carefully stepped through the bushes, at each step searching for something with outstretched leg. Now the other one warned him to take care, and he crawled warily down a fissure between the bushes. The older Gypsy crawled after him, about twelve foot down, and both of them were standing in a rocky hollow about twelve foot long and six foot wide. A sandy rock towered around them, and here pale starlight fell into the hollow through a small central aperture above. Around the rocky wall, there burgeoned a dense elder. On the right, the young Gypsy parted the elder branches, and crawled through a small breach in them into a dark cave. Wherever they stood, they felt soft dry moss everywhere underfoot.

'This is the place,' said the young Gypsy.

'They are well-hidden quarters,' replied the older Gypsy. 'How did you find out about them?'

'Five years ago, when we parted company with your regiment in Hungary, Ligán showed me this hiding-place,' replied the younger man, and putting down his musical instrument, placed his cloak on the ground. 'I don't know how he came to know about it; – we stayed a whole week in it, going out into the neighbouring villages in the daytime.'

'But you went off into eastern lands,' responded the older man, 'and it was from there that you came back.'

'We went off towards the north, and in those northern parts we turned in a semicircle towards eastern lands,' asserted the young Gypsy, spreading out his cloak on the soft moss and lying down on it.

'That is impossible,' replied the older Gypsy, also lying down. 'It is impossible that you could have returned from so long a journey in that time. And none of you ever said that you had been in those parts.'

'No one ever asked us,' replied the younger Gypsy. 'And although we spent time here, we did not delay our journey; but we hastened, continually on the move, so that we might draw level with you in Hungary.'

'Strange,' continued the older Gypsy, lying close to the entrance of the cave, 'strange that Ligán never spoke of this hiding-place to our band, for he was in duty bound to do so.'

'Undoubtedly,' said the younger man, 'he thought that no description could have been adequate for finding this cave, or he thought that everyone who wished to find this hiding-place would have had to have been taken there previously.'

The older Gypsy made a show of believing this, although quite other thoughts were crowding into his mind. 'But why did you bring me here?' he asked the younger man, and raising his head, he turned towards him. 'Tomorrow we shall be travelling onwards, onwards – and doubtless we shall never arrive in this region again.'

The younger Gypsy, suppressing a deep sigh, replied ponderously: 'Who knows whether members of your band might not travel into this region, when I am no longer with you; who would then lead you to this hiding place? – Who knows whether you yourself might need a safe place to lay your head –'

'You are right!' cried the old Gypsy loudly, 'you are right! When I achieve my goal – when I avenge – Ha! Listen! Someone spoke!'

'It is your own voice, echoing in this long, high cave.'

'Quiet! – Listen – again!' – and indeed a dark, hollow voice could be heard, as if someone were speaking from afar, or trying to articulate words from sleep. The Gypsies listened in silence. 'Cold the night!' spoke the hollow voice more clearly, after a pause, 'cold – cold, in your deathly bed!' It fell silent, and its echo resounded yet more hollowly from the high roof. 'Cold the night! – it is your night! – tomorrow the night will be mine!' continued the disquieting voice, now closer to them, as if in a dream, and there was something very terrifying in its tone.

'Who speaks, in this dark lair?' cried the young Gypsy.

'A voice has entered sleep in the den of vengeance, so that the moon's ray may not discover it!' answered the voice slowly.

Each word followed the previous word laboriously, the voice seeming to speak from slumber throughout.

'Light a fire, Giacomo!' said the young Gypsy, giving him dry tinder he had brought for the purpose, and he crept out of the cave to collect more dry kindling.

'Yes, light a fire – it is too cold, here – here – here – as in your heart – alas! – But no – no – light no fire, for it might awaken the moon's ray – and – then –', in a whisper, as if the voice was impatient to fall asleep once more, it continued, 'then they might spy and thwart our love – Ah!' These words were uttered so dully and feebly that the Gypsies would barely have made them out, if a clattering outside, caused by the Gypsy's crawling, had not in any case prevented this.

'Sit closer – thus! – How the waters roar! – O how your hand is cold! –' enjoined the voice. Meanwhile, the younger Gypsy returned with wood, and the older Gypsy, rubbing the kindling together, prepared a fire.

4

Lutuwer: *Sire, the night draws on.*
We must leave.
Mindowe: *Yes, indeed! The moon has set.*
I shall go: perhaps the night air will refresh me.

JULIUSZ SŁOWACKI
Mindowe, King of Lithuania, act III, scene 1 (1832)

WHILE THE GYPSIES were still at the inn, old Bárta was staggering through the valley in the darkness of the night to the castle, which lay about half an hour's walk from the inn. He whiled away the journey with his narrative about the campaign against the French; whenever one of his companions fell, wounded, in his story, he too stumbled and fell – until finally, in his stumbling and falling, he had the misfortune to roll down the hillside to the lake. Down there, however, luckily catching hold of a clump of alders, he fell only knee-deep in the water. While he was rolling down the hill, the bell in the castle rang for the second time. Forcing himself to his feet, he ran and hastened as fast as he could, and shouted and cried; then he fell silent, and once more, slowly staggering, continued his narration about the Napoleonic wars. When he arrived at the castle, the gate had long been locked. – It was not the first time that this had happened, and for this reason he had not been missed in the castle by anyone at all; and for his part he too soon made himself ready. Placing his hat under his head, he lay down against the castle wall, covered his face with his scarf, and, mumbling something about the Rhine, quickly fell asleep. The whole castle was silent – except that a light was burning in the lord's apartment, directly above the sleeping Bárta, and the unmistakable step of the lord, pacing back and forth, could be heard through the open windows.

Dreaming about the French war, Bárta was awakened by the night-watchman's horn from the village below, and the announcement that midnight had struck. Although he wanted to say something, he was checked by the voice of his master. This was Valdemar Lomecký, count of Bork, late captain in the imperial infantry; clearly framed at the window, he was now sighing anxiously into the gloomy night. Bárta, startled, pressed himself against the wall, checking his breathing, so that his lord would not see him and find he had not slept in the castle. Fortunately the night was quite dark.

'Angelina!' cried the lord, 'Angelina! The vengeance foretold in prophecy is come – I sense it – woe is me – alas – all oppresses me! Emma!' – he continued, mopping his brow, and his voice showed that he did not suppose that he was thinking aloud anything that he would not have confided to the desolate night – 'Emma! – if it were only possible to return again; – I – the guilty one – doubted you, the innocent one, and you prophesied vengeance on me, – all of them – Judith – Leah – all of them!' The night-watchman announced midnight a second time; the sound of his horn resounded in the distance over the landscape, and carried up to the castle – for the castle lay not in the dale already described, but above the valley, on a low mound in the middle of the plain. To the east, not far below it, lay a small hamlet, and isolated pinpricks of light shone through the dark shadows of the trees in the gardens encircling it, no doubt because the inhabitants were making their preparations for the next day's celebration.

The lord closed his window; the candles were extinguished, and once more deep silence reigned. In the hamlet, too, one light after another went out, and soon there was not a sign of human life in the whole landscape. For a good while, Bárta did not dare even to open his eyes, for fear that his lord might see him. Finally, plucking up courage, he opened one eye and peered out, and seeing that all was dark above, and that all around was silent, he sat down on the grass and slowly contemplated his lord's words. As he spoke, he gazed at the nocturnal landscape spread out before him. Cold dew was falling on the fields, and here and there mists and nocturnal vapours were drifting over the distant mountains. The stars twinkled with pale rays; from time to time one disappeared, and azure sparks fell on the dark earth. Here and there, pale will-o'-the-wisps played over a swamp in distant forests. In the pond of the village below the frogs were croaking, and from time to time a watchdog barked, with dogs in remoter villages barking in response. Bárta's teeth were chattering from the cold as he ruminated on his lord's words. 'Angelina!' he said, under his breath, 'Angelina? – that was the name of the former landlady – aye – aye – yes – yes, the old lady – no – no – that would be a lie, she wasn't yet old then – no; and Emma? – who would that Emma be? – Now that big portrait that hangs in the blue room next to my lord's room – yes – on my word – that one with that tearful face, they call it Emma; – yes, just the other day the chambermaid asked me to dust the cobwebs off my lady Emma, – yes, and it was from that picture; – my lord never goes into that room, that blue one, and there is nothing but cobwebs there – yes – I know it, I know it all, very well. – But who is the Emma in that picture? – is she a lady? – doubtless she is, even if she's not hanging there next to my lord – well now – perhaps no one knows about that – I don't, either! – And what else? – I think he also pronounced the name of the Jew's daughter? – aye – aye! Leah? or is that wrong? – now who would – now – now, where had I got to?' – At that point, there flared out of the bushes in the hill opposite him, above the valley, the red light of a fire, in a long, narrow beam; clear at its base, it dwindled as it rose higher and higher until finally it merged with the nocturnal darkness. Bárta was cold, and although he had not yet sobered up very much, he was able to remember meeting the Gypsies at the inn that evening, and to recall that such men often spend nights out in the open, or in forests, in front of fires. He also imagined that this would be the case here, and that he might be able to get himself warm. Instantly deciding to go to them, he forced his heavy eyes open, rose, and staggered after the beam. For about a quarter of an hour he tottered on, muttering all kinds of things. Immensely drowsy, he struggled up a hill over the valley, – he looked out, – and all at once the beam vanished, leaving nothing but darkness all around. – Bárta staggered down the hill, tripped, and fell in the moss under a brier; no sooner had he done this than he fell asleep again, and now he did not waken until he was roused by 'the rosy dawn of a new day'.

The source of that beam of light was, as the veteran had correctly discerned, the fire made by the Gypsies. They had not lit the fire to burn through the night, however, but, as we already know, so that they could see the location of the voice which had answered them in the cave, and whose it was. It was fortunate for the veteran that that fire had gone out: he would certainly have made the rest of his way in vain, searching for the source of the light, for even if he had climbed the rock from which the beam was emerging, he would not have been able to reach the fire, for its light was coming through a tiny crevice in the roof of the cave, about ten or fifteen inches wide and long.

The Gypsies did not know of this crevice. Although the light of the fire had broken through outside, the starlight had not penetrated inside the cave even to the slightest degree; and the Gypsies were taking care to ensure that they did not give away their presence in the rocks, or their hiding-place. But while the red light outside was betraying their presence, let us follow what was happening inside the cave.

When the twigs, rubbed together, and the chips of kindling began to generate sparks, the younger Gypsy added a little dry hay, which immediately flared up in a clear flame. They added dry twigs, and a cheerful fire was soon blazing, clearly illuminating the whole cave. – It was an extensive, almost square cave; its walls were mostly smooth, though on its roof there were many holes, overgrown with moss or thick bushes, and well hidden by roots that crept down into the cave. Only one of these holes was open, that through which the red firelight had penetrated. The ground was strewn with dry moss; in the walls around it there were niches, carved out by human hand, and on the ground around it there were stone steps. On one of these steps burned the fire lit by the Gypsies.

The voice which had been speaking ceased; – terrible and lifeless was the silence, only a bird of the night occasionally greeting the midnight hour from afar with its hollow croak. The enormous shadows of the Gypsies flickered on the walls of the cave, illumined in red, and on its high roof. Turning towards the side from which the voice had first come, the young Gypsy peered into a dark corner, where there appeared to be a smaller cave; but he could make nothing out, owing to the darkness prevailing there.

'Come out! Who are you, speaking to us from your lair?' cried the Gypsy. – 'Extinguish the moon!' – replied the voice from the dark corner, 'extinguish the moon! – What do you want? – what of the child? – me? and the girls? me? me? – Not I – it was he! – it was he! – Ah, the moon, the moon! – he comes down to me – with a long – pale hand – with his rays I am with child, child! – Extinguish the moon! – What of the girls? –' The voice came near, and from the dark corner there emerged the wizened figure of a woman in the ruddy light.

Torn and ragged garments hung from her, for clearly she had lost both clothing and mind in her lair; and thin, unkempt, grey locks fell over her wrinkled brow and her mutilated face. Fearful was the expression on her face; deep wrinkles formed dark shadows on her face, illumined in the red light, a deep scar ran across her right cheek, across to the ear, and her half-closed mouth was almost entirely toothless. Her eyes were tightly closed as she crept slowly forward, holding her hand out before her. Her whole figure was bathed in the ruddy glow, which made her appearance yet more terrible. Far behind her stretched her shadow, which grew larger as she approached, until she cast the whole cave into darkness, now standing close to the flame. 'The girls!' she continued, in a rasping voice, her finger pointing at her bare head, 'the girl who warms herself in the moon's ray, for whom water drips from her long black tresses, I know her not, not I – it was he! it was he! The girl who wears a black strip at her throat, who lifts up her infant with that deep wound in her thin breast? I know her not, not I, it was he – it was he! – Ha, ha! the ruined girl! do you think to tell me something new? – ha, ha, ha! –' Thus she spoke, as she slowly approached, fearful fabrications and fearful truths alternating in her words. Now she emerged into the light itself.

'Stay!' cried the younger man, seizing her outstretched hands, 'stay!'

She on whom hands had been laid stopped, opened her eyes, and seeing the stranger, fell to the floor of the cave – on to the soft moss. 'Not I! not I!' she cried, in a sorrowful voice, 'it is he, it is he!'

'Who is "he"?' asked the Gypsy.

'Not I, not I! I am only a poor madwoman – have mercy on my nakedness! I am a beggar-woman, a poor woman – aye! aye! – a poor woman! – Did I say madwoman? it is he! – it is he! – Not I – O I am hungry! O immense hunger! I freeze, so icy, icy! Not I, not I!' –

Something rustled and cried out below the cave; the younger Gypsy quickly went out, but returned immediately.

'It was a bird,' he said, 'I think an owl came in here following the light, which can be seen above through a crevice. We must put out the fire, or we shall give away our hiding-place.'

They were unable to discover anything further from the madwoman; she responded to every question only with 'Not I! Not I! It was he!', and could in no way be induced to give any other answer. The young Gypsy, wrapping her in his cloak, shivering with the cold as she was, gave her some bread which he had brought with him from the inn. Covering herself from head to toe in the cloak that was offered her, she crawled into her dark sleeping-place, continuously repeating, 'Not I – not I!'.

The Gypsies extinguished the fire, and lay down on the soft moss by the entrance to the cave. In her dark corner, the madwoman continued to sit for a long while, ravenously eating the bread they had given her, and repeating disjointed words about the ray of the moon, besides again crying 'Not I, not I!', as if from slumber. The Gypsies no longer heard her; for, exhausted by their journey and their adventures, they were sleeping soundly, even now that midnight was long past. But the madwoman, after keeping silence for a short time, began to speak once more as if from slumber. – Fearful her figure – terrible her face, – and yet even in her delirium it was love that she was celebrating. – Some of her words blended, under her breath, into a song, and finally, in a gentle whisper, her rasping voice repeated this song without waking the sleeping gypsies.

Lo, little boat, rocked on the tide,
O my dear darling!
lover comes drifting, embracing his bride,
O my dear darling!

Far, far has he drifted, borne by the wave,
O my dear darling!
Fathoms of ocean he has for his grave,
alas, dear darling.

Ever more quietly, quietly, she repeated her song, and in the elder bushes in front of the cave, too, a lonely nightingale warbled her words.

5

IT WAS NOW full morning, and a bright beam of daylight
penetrated through the crevice into the cave. It extended over
the pale pillar at the cave's entrance and fell on the dark cave
wall. The nightingale which had been singing in the elder bush
in front of the cave from midnight was now silent, and other
birds began to chatter noisily. A fresh breeze wafted into the
cave, and caressed the locks on the brow of the young Gypsy,
who had just awoken from strange dreams.

He had been dreaming that he had been searching for his
mother, and that she had suddenly disappeared just as he

was about to find her. No one had been able to tell him about her, and he had been so tormented with grief that he himself had finally been unable to tell where he came from, when he had had a mother, or what she had been like, and no one else had known who he was; weeping and solitary, he had wandered through distant forests. In the dream, Leah, the daughter of the old Jew, had embraced him in his grief, and had pointed to her cottage, saying, 'There is your homeland!' He had wept like an infant at her breast – and indeed, as he awoke, there were still tears on his cheek. He sensed a mysterious affinity with Leah, who today seemed more dear, more worthy of love, than she had done on the previous day.

He rose, and in the pale light of day could observe everything around him, though indistinctly as yet. The cloak he had lent to the madwoman during the night lay in front of him; the old Gypsy had also already left the cave. Taking up the cloak, he went out into the bright morning. The lilac emitted a powerful scent, and drops of dew glittered brightly on the surrounding bushes, and on the green floor of the rocky hollow. Among the bushes sat the old Gypsy, impatiently waiting for the younger man to awake, and for them to depart. To his question about the madwoman, the old Gypsy replied that she had woken before him and had wished to leave, and he had been surprised at the ease with which she was able to crawl out over the rocks. Picking up their musical instruments, which were lying in the bushes under a rocky recess, they crawled up and emerged by a thick branch on to the side of the rock. – The whole landscape lay before them in the light of morning – the entire beautiful dale, with its densely overgrown rocks, with its lake, its ruined castle on the rocks opposite, with its isolated cottages, all the distant plain, with its forests, all its fields, its castle at the entrance to the valley. All this lay spread out before the gaze of the Gypsies, in a rosy glow. – In the fields there was already a bustle; country folk were hurrying from all directions along the footpaths to the nearby small town. Its steeples on the western side towered out of a thick cluster of trees behind a pine grove, and their bells were summoning the people to Mass in solemn tones. The younger Gypsy sighed deeply, and they crawled hurriedly down the rocks over the stone levels, so that they would not be noticed by anyone, and so that their hiding-place would not be revealed – if this had not already been brought to light by the madwoman. They returned by the way they had come the previous day, and, emerging through the narrow route from this city of rocks, they overheard a voice declaiming behind a low hillock: 'Ah! – what a night that was! on my word – completely dark – or not completely dark, because some of it was red – and what a red! – and it stretched out like the long blazing tail of a comet, like a fiery broom – aye, aye.' Immediately, a host of young voices screamed 'aye, aye!' at full volume; after they had quietened down again, the rough voice which had been speaking was still to be heard, repeating the 'aye, aye' several times to itself.

Coming out on to the hillside, the Gypsies saw the old veteran Bárta sitting on a small hummock under a dog-rose bush. Round him there were gathered children of both sexes and of assorted sizes, some sitting, some standing, some smaller children holding hands, and so forth. There were many dog-roses blooming on the high slopes around, and their powerful scent wafted down over the whole dewy valley.

'And here we are – meanwhile I'm unsheathing the sabre –'
– 'And where's the sabre?' asked the children.

Bárta quickly reached down by his side, but the sabre was not in its sheath. He had to think for some time before he remembered that he had thrown it on to the table in the Jews' garden, in front of the Gypsies, the previous day, and then, losing the thread, he shouted loudly, 'Be damned! It's on the stone table in the Jews' garden!'

'And how did it get there,' asked one of the boys, 'if you were unsheathing it here?'

'Ah, be damned!' cried Bárta, 'when I unsheathed it, it flew out of my hands!'

– 'So did it fly into the Jews' garden?' asked the children. 'Yes, into the Jews' garden!' repeated Bárta, 'straight on to the stone table!'

– 'But how did you see it, if the night was so dark?' demanded his listeners.

'Eh – ah – its tail was glowing, that light, yes, yes, and now just be quiet and don't muddle me, and listen! – so I unsheathe that sabre – yes, that sabre, – so that I could kill that dragon which was wanting to destroy our beloved neighbourhood, for it was nothing but a fiery dragon –; there's nothing else that has a tail like that, a tail like a long-shield – aye – aye! –' Once more his listeners all shouted out his 'aye, aye', and finally the old veteran, as if echoing them, loudly repeated his 'aye – aye' several more times.

The Gypsies drew nearer, listening to his story.

'And here I tripped, and I flew downhill this way, the dragon took fright, hid his tail, and disappeared, and I fell down – ha, ha, ha!' The whole dale resounded with the 'ha, ha, ha!' laughter of the listening children; after they were quiet once more, the old veteran, still echoing their laughter, continued with his story: 'It was freezing in the morning; in the morning I sit down, I huddle down, yes, on my word, I huddle down and I sit, and I stay – and I stay sitting there; or no – no, that'd be a lie, because now I get up, and I'm going, and I'm going – and I'm going –'

'– To the inn!' they all shouted in unison, for it was the usual conclusion to all Bárta's stories. 'To the Jews' inn!' confirmed Bárta, and pulling himself to his feet, he strode off to the place in question. The Gypsies joined him, and all three disappeared along the footpath in the rocks. The children went on shouting 'aye – aye!' after them for some time, and each time they stopped, Bárta repeated his habitual 'aye – aye' after them.

When they had already gone some distance down between the rocks, and no longer had to prise apart the bushes and squeeze under the branches of the birches, the younger Gypsy asked Bárta whether he knew who the madwoman was, whom they had met the previous night among the rocks. Bárta, immediately ready to tell his tale, sat down on a low stone, twirled his moustache, and began: 'Ah – I know, I know it all, very well indeed. The madwoman – was she short and bent? No? – That was our mad beggar-woman. –'

The Gypsies preferred that he should tell them about it as they walked, so Bárta rose; and positioning himself with the younger Gypsy in front and the older one behind him, ordered them to keep in step along the narrow path, so that they could both hear. Then he began to tell his story very loudly: 'In a fortnight, it will be just a year since she moved here with her husband from somewhere or other. Aye – on my word, that was a strange man, as strange as – yes; and so was she. He'd also been a soldier, loved talking, was cheerful, like me – only he was one who used to wander all day from one inn to another, drunk almost all the time, ha, ha, ha! – But I'll tell you something – yes – and no one knows about this, unless they've heard it from me. – Yes, everyone thought it was her husband, – though then she wasn't yet mad – but – as ugly as sin, yes – scarred, a mutilated face – oh, her whole body, as people thought – but me – I – be damned – I kept my eye on the whole affair. He wasn't her husband – aye – aye – yes – so he wasn't, he just kept in with her, because I think she had money, and he needed it, as he told me once in the inn. – She wanted to be with him, for him to appear to be her husband, – he didn't know why – no one knows why, and I don't either! and later I think she bought the cottage here. – Yes, even at that time she was strange; I think she had mutilated her face herself – he told me all about it. It's said she used to sit in the cottage all day but always go walking above in the valley at night, there by the charnel stone, and every night there – no – no, that'd be a lie, not every night, but only when the moon was out, yes – and they say she used to say strange things. And it's said the moon – be damned – yes, the moon, he used always to wander around there, and it's said he begot a child with her, with a long finger as white as snow, and when she didn't go to the charnel stone, it's said he always came in to her through the window, and then they say everyone was able to see it. But no one, no one saw it, and I didn't see it either. – Six months after that, her husband died, no – not her husband – but the man who was with her, just when she had lost everything except for some debts to be settled in the inn and in the neighbourhood. – They forced her out of the cottage, and she had nothing to live on. She had nothing at all left, not a farthing. – More and more out of her mind as time went on, she used to go during the day to the charnel stone – and sit there under the ancient oak, begging from passers-by – and she always disappeared during the night. Later she never sat under the ancient oak when the moon was shining – no, never – because she became terrified of its light. I know all this well – very well. Once I was going home from the town near here; it was late at night – and overcast – terrifying – aye, yes, terrifying. I went through the forest, around the charnel stone, – it was dark, and I – no – no – that would be a lie, no – I never trembled – never! – But I go on and on, until I get to the Jew– – eh, – no, until I get to the ancient oak. I'm going slowly, and taking care not to bump into any trees. Then a beggar's voice is raised close to me; I'm – no, no, that would be a lie, I'm not scared, and I try to walk on further. Suddenly the clouds break – and straight above me, yes, straight above me there's the moon, and in front of me, under the ancient oak, stands the madwoman – and she starts screaming – and she runs – runs, throws herself on the earth, and scrabbles with her nails in the earth, and covers her face with it, and I race away, with those screams behind me – and I race away through the forest – until, ha, ha, ha! what? – Wherever had I got to? – oh, yes – now she's completely crazed, yes, completely. During the day, as usual, she goes begging, sitting by the charnel stone, and at night she always disappears – yes – be damned – she's gone. People round here give her a wide berth, for it's said that if she talks to anyone, they will certainly have bad fortune.'

During this speech, they crossed the stream and went up along the footpath to the inn. Leah stood by the fence of the little garden looking down towards them, her eyes and lips seeming to smile. 'Aye, aye,' marvelled the veteran, looking up at her, and could find no words except 'aye – aye' to answer the Gypsies when they asked why he was so surprised. They entered the little garden. Leah ran to meet them, and embraced the younger of them, gazing steadily into his dark blue eyes. 'Stay with us!' she cried in a pleading voice, 'stay with us; we too are aliens in this land; our lodging place will be your lodging place with us. My father has given his consent, yes – he desires it. Stay with us!' The older Gypsy trembled at these words, as if the single word 'stay' was strangely affecting his whole existence. The young Gypsy, surprised – not, however, by Leah's conduct, but by the fact that his dreams were reaching fulfilment – gazed into her beautiful face, unable to say a word.

The old veteran, continually repeating his 'aye – aye', owing to his unbounded amazement, had not even managed to order his glass of liquor; hearing the bell from the castle summoning him as usual, he quickly shouted for a drink, hastily drained it as it was brought, hurriedly rose, and left immediately, disappearing in the cowsheds beyond the stream while uttering nothing but 'aye – aye!' –

'Will you stay with us?' Leah repeated her question, in a pleading voice. The young Gypsy had loved Leah already the previous day, for her solicitude, before setting eyes on her; his dream had heightened the suddenly kindled love; the sight now of her beautiful face made it seem that he could never bid her farewell.

She was standing before him in the same Oriental costume as on the previous day; her black tresses emphasized the sweet pallor of her tender face; and her dark eyes, today for the first time smiling, had not yet lost their longstanding melancholy; and it seemed to the young Gypsy, viewing the ancient ruins of the fortress on the right, and the sandy rocks lit up in the rosy morning light on the left, that these belonged to the features of this, the most beautiful of the daughters of Zion, smiling through her tears over the ruins of a deserted Jerusalem.

He was a youth also handsome of face, even though his figure was unprepossessing and his bearing defective. His black locks and dark moustache adorned a magnificent, distinguished countenance, which, burnt by the sun to a reddish-brown through his long travels, bore a melancholy though engaging smile. All his conduct, every movement he made revealed immense vivacity, and the occasional, almost savage, flash of his dark blue eyes showed that his love could be sought, and was equally to be feared; yet this is something that always kindles yet greater love in the heart of a girl. His face radiant, he gazed into Leah's eyes, and her gaze became warm in the dark depths of his eyes.

'Stay with us!' pleaded Leah; he loved her, and yet there seemed to be something drawing him away. 'Stay with you?

am I to stay here?' he cried, in a mournful, grieving voice, 'with you? – O how gladly I would do so! – There is no place to which my longing draws me; my race knows no homeland for which its heart might yearn! – Am I to stay here? – Everything attracts me here; here it seems as if every tree-trunk, every rock knows me, and can speak to me of ancient times and of the days of my childhood! – And – yet –'

'Stay with us!' pleaded Leah, 'why continue to yearn and seek, when you say that everything attracts you?' The old Jew also approached, beseeching him to remain, and in his plea his miserliness and his love for his daughter fought a strange battle. He ended with the words, 'Here will be our tabernacle, here will be our dwelling-place! – Long may the desires of my grey hairs be fulfilled, that I may dwell with you and safeguard my fortune with you! And when the days draw nigh that I shall die and sleep with my fathers, and my dust will be trampled underfoot in a strange land, who will there be to shelter this unhappy daughter of Israel, who will care for the fortune which her father has amassed through the vicissitudes of this life?' – Each time he spoke of his fortune, he glanced around apprehensively in case anyone other than the Gypsy was overhearing this declaration, and each time his voice dropped so low that even the Gypsy could not hear his words. 'No one knows her heart,' he continued, 'no one understands what weighs upon it! No one can measure her pain except those who wander like us, far removed from their homeland. Who will take charge of this poor daughter of Zion, when her father sleeps and is called into Abraham's bosom? Our nation is held in contempt, no rights are afforded to the stranger! Who will defend this child of a deserted Jerusalem from dishonour? Like wolves in a desolate mountain range they lie in wait for us,' he whispered fearfully, 'to steal the lambskin from us. My child has trust in you; the secrets of your heart were revealed yesterday among us. You too are an orphan; your dispersed nation does not recognize its own son; there is no one to attend with kindness to your steps through your desolate pilgrimage. You are accustomed to be patient, you are content with few things. My daughter loves you! –'

Leah had been holding the Gypsy in a tight embrace, as if she were afraid that he might refuse her father's request and slip from her arms. But, looking upon Leah's pale, tearstained face, he slid to his knees in the colourful blossoms at her bare feet, and, clasping her, cried, with an ardour unusual in his nation, 'Leah, do you love me?'

'Yes – yes!' replied Leah, bending over to him, and, kneeling, they joined in an ardent embrace.

'O if your love could encompass the height of my affection!' groaned the Gypsy. 'Only the depth of my grief can equal the height of my love,' replied Leah.

'That deep grief seized the heart of my daughter,' said the old Jew, standing before them, 'as the cold waters of Cedron enshroud the Mount of Olives in chill mists; and the flood of her tears is like the great fountain of the pool of Siloah, gushing forth in a rocky valley: but your future has driven away the mists from the palms at the Jordan, and her tears are dews on the scattered roses of Jericho.'

'Leah! my dearest! my bride!' cried the Gypsy.

'Stay with us!' repeated Leah.

'Then, narrow rocks, take me into your embrace and tend me silently in your pleasant cradle; young saplings, whisper in my dreams, lull my heart to sleep, soothe my grief!' Sunk in deep musing, the Gypsy poured out his lament into the blossoming dale in these words.

'My final years will be filled with joy,' spoke the Jew, clasping his trembling hands in gratitude, 'and when I am old and grey-headed, I will not be forsaken. Now you will no longer be desolate like the turtle-dove in the deserts of Arabia, you will rejoice on the blossoming hills like a roe or young hart upon the mountains of Bether, and your voice will be like a cluster of camphire in the vineyards of Engedi. – Your name will be blessed among us; all around are the dwellings of the rich, and your name will be exalted with music, like a cedar of Lebanon!'

'Stay with us!' pleaded Leah.

'Yes, yes! I will stay with you! Where could my pilgrimage bring me? Into an empty, heartless world, with none to know my sorrows, to understand my heart, to console! – Here is my homeland, my fatherland, my own country! here love greets me, graciousness holds me, sympathy prevails! – Yes, I will remain here, with you!'

The older Gypsy, taking up his musical instrument, turned away from them, saying, 'Farewell!' As he left the little garden, his countenance lit up with expressions of strange emotion. His wrinkled face displayed traces of longing, of love, of vengefulness; and many other passions competed in it in a fearful blend, in a strange contest with his greying whiskers and locks.

'Do not leave us!' cried the younger man, running after him and, seizing his hands, holding him back, 'are you wishing to leave us here, where I have hopes of finding what I have craved so long?'

'Away, away! my longing and my vengeance know no stay, no rest, no repose!' – replied the older Gypsy.

'You have been searching so long in vain, and now you still hope to find what you have never found. You have been my father!' –

'Precisely because I have sought so long in vain, the longing for vengeance remains alive in me; kindled to the highest degree, it urges me ever onward.'

'In your old age –'

'Precisely because there are not many days of life left to me, there is all the more need of labour to achieve the long desired goal! Away, away, to –'

'My father, do you remember the night when I first came to you? An abandoned child, I was wandering through a dense forest; from afar off the fires glowed like stars of hope; I ran to find them. Around the fires sat an unknown throng. It was the Gypsy race. Weak in the rain as I was, you wrapped me in your cloak and welcomed me to the fire. As you said, something inexpressible attracted you to me and likewise me to you. You promised me you would not leave me, and I – I could not have done without you. – And now you wish – you wish to leave me? Stay with us!'

The older Gypsy remained silent.

'Free every day to go off into the neighbourhood – also to stay away for longer periods, only provided you always come back to us!' The older man still remained silent. 'Who knows whether here you may not find –'

The older Gypsy trembled; like a lightning bolt, a shaft of emotion flashed across his face, and as if he had already thought about this previously, he cried: 'Have you noticed? do you think so? – ah, no – you do not know! – but yes, I shall remain!' – He turned round, picked up his violin, took the cloak of the younger man, since he had no cloak of his own; and vaulting over the fence, hastened into the dale, up through the valley, and disappeared around a bend in the rocks.

6

– 'O that he might suffer eternally,
he who is the cause of my damnation!
May endless ages not quench hell with his tears,
and may he never gain the bliss of heaven,
as I too cannot...'

SEWERYN GOSZCZYŃSKI
Sobótka (1834)

THUS THE GYPSIES remained in that place. During the day, they wandered into neighbouring villages and inns according to their accustomed way of life, and by night the younger Gypsy used to return to the Jews' cottage, where, from that evening, his life began to be more cheerful; the older Gypsy, however, made different, mysterious journeys even during the night. The old veteran, Bárta, patronized the inn every evening as he had done previously, and, habitually cheerful even when they were miserable, it is not hard to imagine that he did not turn miserable now that they had become more cheerful than they had been before. The old Jew, the serving girl and he – in a word, everyone – loved the younger Gypsy; the behaviour of the older one, however, even though he was seldom to be seen, excited a mysterious horror in all of them. The young Gypsy loved Leah with his whole heart and with all the ardour of young love, as was possible only in a young Gypsy, fiery by blood and upbringing, who for the first time had encountered someone with the same feelings as his own. It may be that there was yet another reason for his ardent love, which will emerge more clearly later in the unfolding of this tale. Leah loved him similarly, and for the same reasons, and grew more cheerful day by day – or so it seemed.

But the Gypsy's immense jealousy intruded on his own contentment, and also on hers. It is frequently to be observed that the more ardent the passion of a lover, the more fiery his jealousy. That was also the case here. Leah's occasional melancholy aroused the Gypsy's deepest suspicion, and the occasional words she exchanged with another of the residents in the cottage, whose purpose he could not fathom, fuelled his apprehensions. On one such occasion he hounded Leah with agitated words; she swore that she loved no one but him, and assured him that he was the only one who had won her love. After this exchange, her earlier melancholy once more clouded her face, and the Gypsy, realizing that his doubts were the cause of this grief, begged for her forgiveness, weeping, and promising that he would never doubt her again. This was in vain; the very next day, another inconsequential word would rekindle his jealousy, and a petty thought would cast him back into an unquenchable flame of terrible doubts.

It was about three weeks after their arrival that the Gypsies took leave of each other one evening, going their separate ways, each for his own purpose. The younger Gypsy, going through the deep dale and the dense pine forest towards the Jews' cottage, came to the ancient oak by the charnel stone.

This level area is the most extensive in a valley that is, in all, several miles long, but otherwise very narrow. On the right-hand side, there is a steep hill overgrown with tall pines; at its heel, strongly raging, is an invisible stream, which, bursting out of the extensive rocks, falls into dense, low bushes. The spacious area is circular, entirely overgrown with moss, and, except for the narrow entrance at the left, densely overgrown all around with bushes, over which stand tall, supercilious pines. A broad, sandy path leads through the middle. Divided in the middle of the flat area around the broad old oak, this again joins in a single broad path beyond it. The oak, though spreading, is not tall, but hunchbacked, bent over towards the earth out of which it has grown. Of immense age, it is now entirely hollow, and its bark, riddled with holes and charred in places, assumes terrible shapes. Its crown is entirely bent towards the west over a low rock overgrown with moss; but towards the east there are only two long branches, each ending with greenery, so that it seems as if two long, crooked, misshapen arms are reaching out forward, presenting a garland. Under them, in the hollow bark, is fashioned a ghastly human face, whose inburnt hollow eyes glitter blue in the dark night with rotting material. Under this face there is a large hollow in the oak, like the hidden lair of a wild animal, and long white moss hangs before it like the long beard of a fearful face. Within this hollow there is a sandy rock, carved out like a seat, and entirely overgrown with moss. It is the seat of the mad beggar-woman.

From this oak, a second, narrower path on the left leads to a narrow aperture, beyond which stands the charnel stone, extremely massive and overgrown with bushes. It is a large, sandy rock, towering about three foot above the bushes, on which there have been carved, by rain – and perhaps by the hand of humans – the likenesses of human bones and skulls, and I imagine it is from them that it has been given its name. Anyone who would wish to go by this footpath was obliged to crawl over this rock. Further beyond the rock there was a narrow footpath, and further again – the higher it went – a broader one. This path led up higher and higher between sandy rocks, also apparently strewn with skulls and bones, into a dense forest above. Close to the skulls of these rock walls there were green bushes, waving like feathers on a helmet, or red flowers, called Tears of the Virgin, wreathing the bald skulls.

This path was little used, an indication that few were bold enough to choose this route. Especially at night, no one dared to crawl over the charnel stone along this path, and everyone preferred to make a detour of more than half an hour by the broader footpath through the vale. Superstitions were rife about this place, that ghosts walked on this narrow footpath between the high walls strewn with skulls and bones; that the skulls and bones chattered, moving in their places; and that an early death was in store for anyone happening to spy a white figure here.

No one chose this path, especially in recent times, except the old Gypsy, when he wished to meet the younger one, and the madwoman, when she returned from her begging, making her way to her lair.

And, in this place, by the ancient oak, Leah met the Gypsy. It was late evening; it had darkened strongly and suddenly, for the sun had gone down behind thick, black clouds which had risen up in the western sky. The clouds were still edged with a golden glow, but occasional pale lightning traversed them below, where they were resting on the distant mountains, and it was easy to see that after this sultry day a powerful storm was in store for the night.

A strong fragrance stole over the forest, oppressed by the rapidly falling darkness. A deep, lifeless silence prevailed; not even the lightest breeze was stirring the flowers in the high moss and at the bank of the stream. The tall pines stood like dark shadows behind the dense bushes, which edged this plain all round. In the middle stood the old oak in its fearful posture, and in its hollow sat the madwoman, still begging. Fixing her eyes on the two branches stretched out above her, she was whispering incomprehensible words. One could not tell whether she was praying, or whether a mysterious curse was being woven in her words.

Leah, who had been sitting on the flat space by the old oak, ran with a happy cry into the open, out of the dense bushes, to the Gypsy as he entered. She tried to throw her arms around his neck, but, raising his hand, he held it up before her, crying out, 'Get back!' in a deep, trembling voice. It was clear that he had made great haste, for his breast was rising and falling, strongly and quickly, and he was breathing heavily.

'Get back from me!' he exclaimed, 'back! This is what I expected!'

'My dearest!' cried Leah, shocked.

'Why have you come to this place?' asked the Gypsy abruptly.

'I came out to meet you!' replied Leah.

Gypsy: 'Today? – only today? – why not at other times?'

Leah: 'I have never known which way you come back. Yesterday you said – '

Gypsy: 'O indeed! do not shatter my illusions! Leah! –' *(very mournfully)* 'Leah! Why did you lie and say you loved me, why did you not leave me to wander on into the wide world? – I would not have known of the bliss for which I shall now be yearning in vain! –'

Leah: 'Again it is your fantasy –'

Gypsy (wildly): 'Have you nothing to say to me? nothing for which to beg my forgiveness? nothing? –'

Leah: 'I do not know –'

Gypsy: 'Do you not know anything? – Truly? –'

Leah (mournfully): 'Nothing!'

Gypsy: 'Leah!' *(more wildly)* 'Leah! do you not know anything?'

Leah: 'Again you –'

Now the Gypsy's wildness reached its highest level. Taking Leah forcibly by the hand, with blazing eyes he glowered savagely into her pale face, and, his whole body trembling, he cried in a hollow voice: 'O admit only that you did not expect me so soon! Confess! – Leah, who was that man in elegant hunting clothes with a white feather waving on his green hat? A black beard –'

Although Leah had already witnessed other such outbreaks of violent words from him, she trembled with intense horror, and great tears trickled down her pale face.

'A black beard!' repeated the Gypsy, 'he had a double-barrelled gun at his shoulder, and strode up through the forest –'

'Valdemar Lomecký! It is he, it is he! it is not I – not I!' a voice cried out above them. The madwoman was standing above her usual seat, with her hand raised up high, clinging to dead branches.

Without crying out, indeed without a sound or a word, Leah collapsed in the moss under the ancient oak. 'Leah! Leah! O God!' cried the young Gypsy. But, quickly rising to her feet, she ran home. The young Gypsy hurried after her; her white dress was already far away in the gloom. 'Leah! Leah!' cried the Gypsy, racing after her, until his voice could no longer be heard in the distance. –

Whistling to himself, the old Gypsy crawled up the charnel stone after a time, and jumping over it, went after them into the dark undergrowth, paying no attention to anything around him. Howling with laughter, the madwoman remained alone in the dark of the forest.

More and more intensely, darkness engulfed the heart of the deep dale, and the lofty pines around disappeared in the shadows. In the darkness, the ancient oak seemed a ghastly figure seated in the midst of a deserted plain; and, in the raging storm, its two east-facing branches were swaying the most, like long, outstretched hands. The gloomy tempest howled between the charnel walls, across the charnel stone, and the young bushes waved like dark crests on white helmets over the stone skulls. Cackling, the madwoman sat under the swaying branches in the deep darkness, in the hollow of the ancient oak; the hideous face in the bark of the oak gleamed with its rotting eyes in the dark night. She continually whispered dark curses, and, from the depths, distant thunder rolled in the fearful words of her curses. From time to time, a pale lightning flash lit up the broad space faintly, so that the ancient oak, the charnel stone and their surroundings could be half seen; – and night drew on, ever blacker and blacker.

7

Lonely the maiden:
with her gaze and with her sighs
she reaches towards the face of the moon.

She searches the angels in heaven,
beating her white breast with her palms:
'O moon, take me to your bosom,
woe is me in this world!...'

ALEKSANDER DUNIN-BORKOWSKI
Longing (1834)

He whispered, whispered his report – and over the knight's countenance
there spread a black, ever blacker, cloud;
and once more his face, suddenly yet darker with despair,
blazed with anger and disdain, as if with lightning;
until finally a wild fury arose in him,
directed at a single object: the death of his contender;
which might sever the holiest of bonds in the fire of its wrath.
Until finally a frenzied craving arose in him
for blood, screams, bells, flame, issuing from a polluted womb,
which ignites the torches of conjugal discord,
and punishes iniquity with iniquity in its own nest!

ANTONI MALCZEWSKI
Maria, A Ukrainian Romance (1825)

At times the horizon cracked from side to side,
and the angel of the storm, like an immense sun,
showed his glittering face; and again, wrapped in a shroud,
he fled into the sky and the doors of the clouds crashed together
with a thunder-clap.

ADAM MICKIEWICZ
Lord Thaddeus (1834; prose translation by G.R. Noyes, 1917)

NOW DARKNESS began to loom strongly; black clouds rolled in swiftly from the west, and, as if the heavens were falling, dropped down on to the thirsty earth. Thick darkness oppressed the rocks and trees, and stalked around the ruined tower; old Bárta nonetheless sat by the Jews' cottage, now drunk, crossing himself from time to time, while the lightning showed his hands the way to his filled glass, even if occasional 'aye – aye' interjections were gliding out of his throat during his narrative. Looking around at the looming sky and the ruins shrouded in the gloom, he concluded his tale, which had been heard by no one but himself; and today, perhaps for the first time ever, he ended with the formula, 'I go, and I go, until I get – away from the Jews' inn'.

Standing up, putting the glass to his lips, and draining it – in his own words, polishing it off – he staggered out of the little garden. At the wicket gate, a white figure flew towards him. Tottering, he fell over to one side. At the heels of the figure – it was Leah – dashed the young gypsy, desperately crying, 'Leah! Leah! what is amiss?' Leah collapsed in the grass by the stone table. Old Bárta also staggered over to the table, and clinking his glass on the table, gestured towards the recumbent Leah as the serving girl came running. Evidently accustomed to such spectacles, she led her master's daughter across to a turf seat by the stone table, and Leah, her head in her hands, wept bitterly.

'Leah! Leah!' sobbed the Gypsy, kneeling at her feet. His voice was dreadful, as if it were issuing from a withered breast in a deep grave. 'Leah! is it true then? has my yearning then not deceived me? – Leah! only a single word!'

Weeping, she gave him no answer; but he recovered himself, rising abruptly to his feet. A terrible resolve to achieve certainty had altered his behaviour all at once. A strange smile hovered on his lips, like a demonic bolt of lightning; he passed his hands over his brow and over his breast, and then, as if cut short, he asked the serving girl: 'What is the matter with her? – Judith, tell me, what is the matter with her? –'

'I don't know,' answered the girl, 'she was like this formerly, before you came to us; she was formerly like this – but why – I don't know!'

'She was formerly like this!' repeated the Gypsy, 'and was she always so from her infancy?'

'No, no! – she used to be cheerful, more cheerful than I am, but –'

There came an enormous lightning flash, and the whole landscape, previously dark, was lit up. The girl broke off abruptly; but the Gypsy remained immobile, his nails digging into his breast, and his eyes remained glazed and fixed on the girl even in the complete absence of light. Bárta, who had fallen on the grass, strained to get up, but, shouting loudly and crossing himself, fell once more. Meanwhile, Leah, rising to her feet, raised her eyes and her hands imploringly towards the girl, in case she might be too weak to remain upright; but neither the immobile Gypsy, nor the girl, who had turned towards the veteran, noticed her. The lightning vanished, and the darkness became even deeper than it had been previously. 'But, but –' urged the young Gypsy, insistently. 'But once, eight years ago,' continued the girl, 'Angelina, the housekeeper at the castle, came in the evening, and had secret words with my lord, taking Leah away. Where? I don't know –.' Leah sighed deeply; it was like a death rattle. 'Uneasily, we waited for her to return. Her anxious father went out several times in his distress to meet her; – in vain; – each time he returned yet more distraught.'

The Gypsy stood there as if turned to stone. It was as well that the deep darkness was hiding his face, or the terrified girl would have fled before it.

'After midnight,' continued Judith, 'after midnight she came running, alone, with her head uncovered, worn out, raging against herself; half dead, she was lamenting, "Unhappy nation of ours! Who will defend the exile in a strange land?" She said nothing more, and never explained. If anyone remembers that time, her behaviour was as it is today; and from that night, no smile ever graced her pale face; but she used to sit there in front of the cottage, not saying a word, her eyes fixed in the distance, occasionally singing a mournful song to herself.'

'Where had she been – what had she done there – does no one know, – no one at all?' cried the Gypsy, moderating his words owing to the need to maintain quiet. Hot tears were falling on his sunburnt face, and hot blood was oozing from his agitated breast under his clenched fingers. Just then, the ailing old Jew called out in the cottage, and Judith hurried into the low room.

'Does no one know? – every child knows,' began the veteran, on his feet, tottering over to the table and sitting down while speaking, 'yes, every child knows – I've told them myself – I've kept my eye on it all myself. – Though they gave me orders, and I had a beating because I didn't keep quiet, on my word – yes – But even if they were to lay me low again immediately, it would have to come out; and besides, my lord still isn't home yet today, he went over the fields into the town, and he won't be home till – till – morning –'

'So no one knows!' sighed the Gypsy, not noticing Bárta, and he turned as if to leave.

'Hey, hey! stop!' – Bárta seized the Gypsy, afraid that he would miss his story. 'No one knows? – I know – everything –'

'Tell me, tell me what you know, for God's sake!' shouted the Gypsy, startled, clutching at Bárta.

'Oh, yes! hold with me – yes – yes –,' continued Bárta, very disjointedly and incoherently, 'yes – hold with me – anyway, it all depends on me – and my feet give me trouble – yes, from the time that we were on the Rhine, – oh, I knew how to give them the slip then – on my word –'

'Tell me! tell me what you know about Leah!' cried the Gypsy, drawing the staggering Bárta over to the stone table.

'Yes – yes! – I'll explain it to you. – Once I was on my way home; in two months' time it'll be eight years since it happened, I wrote it down. – I'm on my way home from here, because I saw old Angelina taking Leah away, and I wanted to know where they were going; because I've got to know – everything – yes – everything. So I hurry to get home – and it was too late, the gate locked, and me outside, and I couldn't get into the castle at all. And I think to myself, "what now?" – and I lie down on the ground, as I always do when I arrive too late and I can't get into the castle. And there I'm lying, I doze off now and then, and now and then I'm looking down towards the village, where not the slightest light was now to be seen. Above me were my lord's windows – and they were dark too – and silent – silent – no – no, that'd be a lie – not silent; – for suddenly a door slammed so that the window was rattling, I hear a woman scream, the menacing voice of a man, and howling laughter; – it seemed to me it was the old house-keeper – the woman formerly in charge of the inn.'

The Gypsy was standing, oblivious, not hearing or paying attention, but these words roused him from his dreadful imaginings to a dreadful certainty. 'Angelina!' he shouted, and, leaning on the table, brought his head right up to the lips of the veteran, as if his ears were weak and unable to hear all that was being said. Bárta was sitting at the stone table.

Wordlessly, Leah rose, in dreadful mortification. Leaning against the table, she was making a great effort, and her eyes were blazing desperately, as if to stem any further narration. Now and then she raised her right hand pleadingly towards Bárta, whose back was turned towards her; but she dropped it again feebly each time, unable to utter a single word. She had assumed that no one knew about this, for, speaking to no one, she had never heard what Bárta had been telling everyone; and now – it had to be heard by him, the only one she had loved, whose present deadly feelings she could imagine; for she had

71

well grasped his boundless sensitiveness, jealousy, and wildness. Meanwhile, the storm approached nearer and nearer; during the story, there was more frequent lightning, although in the sheer deep darkness, nothing could be made out.

'That lasted some time, – I trembled like an aspen leaf,' continued Bárta, 'for if they had found me and seen that I was not at home – and suddenly the window flies open – terrible screams then – and here Leah flies out of the window – aye – aye, yes, out of the window – be damned – out of the window, sixty foot up – no – no – that'd be a lie – fifty-five, yes, fifty-five, right in front of me, and she runs away. I pulled myself together and hid so that no one would see me. – What happened after that – I don't know – I don't know anything – but I've told you that –'

Leah, mortified, collapsed again in the azure lightning, and dragged herself away to her customary place by the cottage; from time to time, desperate groans welled up from the depths of her agitated heart. After a time the lightning was followed by a terrible crash of thunder; and the rocks continued to repeat its dreadful sound for a long while. The Gypsy no longer heard anything; petrified, he was staring blankly into the sheer darkness, and his hot tears failed to quieten the deep grief in his breast.

'Yes, I talked about it, on my word – and they grabbed me, and I had to admit I had come too late, and they gave me a beating, and ordered me – yes – but my lord isn't at home –'

'And no one, no one stood up –' said the Gypsy under his breath.

'Stood up?' Hearing the last few words, Bárta interrupted. 'Stood up? – For whom? hardly for her – the

Jewess? – yes – I wouldn't have suggested anyone do that; and against whom? – against my lord? – yes – aye – aye – aye –'

'Valdemar Lomecký!' continued the Gypsy.

'Yes, that's what our lord was called – what he is called; – Valdemar Lomecký, count of Bork. – But today, today he isn't at home; he has gone over the fields into the town to visit friends, and he won't be back till tonight, yes, not till tonight. – Tonight? – what's the time now?' – And as if he had just remembered, Bárta looked around him. 'What, is it night already? That's impossible! hey, hey!' Looking for his glass, with which to summon the girl, he tottered around the table and collided with the immobile Gypsy. 'What's that? – who's here?' asked Bárta.

'Valdemar Lomecký!' cried out the Gypsy, in a terrible voice; 'just as the wrath of heaven is assembling over our heads, my revenge will be as swift as its lightning, as terrible as its voice!'

A powerful flash of lightning appeared, lasting for some time. The whole landscape – the dark shadows of the trees, the fearful figures on the rock walls, the tower of the ruined castle, the rock level on the opposite side, the whole dale – blazed in its azure brilliance. – The Gypsy's eyes, overflowing with rage, were half blinded. – Erect before the stone table, his hair standing on end, and raising his right hand to heaven, with his left hand he smashed his musical instrument; its strings snapped, and their dying voice seemed to be speaking. 'Scattered is my nation', came the final echo. Opposite him, at the other table, stood the fearful figure of the madwoman, and at her feet was the old Gypsy. Leah sighed deeply in her porch; and Bárta, falling on the grass, screamed loudly with terror.

'Ha, ha, ha! it is not I! – not I – it is he! – it is he!' cried the madwoman, with her mocking laughter, 'ha, ha, ha! it is he! revenge! revenge! revenge!'

'Revenge!' repeated the old Gypsy, in a hollow voice. Now the lightning ceased, and sheer darkness enveloped the whole dale. Nothing could be seen, and only the deep, rapid breathing of the young Gypsy was echoing in the silence that had overcome the anxious landscape. After a moment, there came an enormous clap of thunder; and 'It is he! it is he!' shouted the madwoman into its terrible crash. 'It is he! not I! not I – ha, ha, ha! that youth! ha, ha, ha! it is he! it is he! he seduced me – I should not have been alone; not I – not I –! he seduced others – I have prepared only revenge for him!' Now the echo of the great thunderclap repeated in the distance. After a time, as if coming to her senses, the madwoman spoke with returning memory: 'It is he! it is he! your bliss was brought to shipwreck by him, mad youth! – I too had been happy in the embrace of my parents, in the embrace of a lover – far – far – ha, ha, ha! – It was he – it was not I – not I! he seduced me, and I seduced him; I was the one who gave her to him; it was I! – what he took from her by force, I sacrificed to him willingly – it was I! – and with that cottage – with that he wished to recompense me – with that – with that – ha, ha, ha!'

'Angelina!' cried out the Gypsy, sinking back on to the stone table.

Once more, bright lightning cast light on this terrible spectacle; loud thunder followed; and deep darkness, deep silence followed again. 'Angelina! yes – yes, I am Angelina,' cried the madwoman. The old Gypsy gave a start, as if wishing to leap to the aid of the younger man; not being able by any means to move, he remained where he was. The younger man fell, writhed on the ground, and, groping for words, emitted incomprehensible sounds. Again there was deep darkness.

'Yes, it was I! it was I!' continued the madwoman, 'yes, I, Angelina, procured your lover for him! – Do you weep? for her – for her? –' and, lost in thought, 'O – perhaps he was also weeping thus for me when the waters rocked his boat under the Rialto Bridge – my Giacomo! – when –'

Again there was a brilliant lightning flash, and the whole landscape was lit up. The hideous figure of the madwoman was still standing at the stone table, her left hand covering her eyes, and her right hand pointing south. Grief-stricken, the young Gypsy drew himself erect, moving his lips soundlessly, and with his right hand he pointed towards his bared breast, on which a birthmark gleamed distinctly in the azure flash of the lightning, like blood-red hands lifted up to make a vow. But the older man, seeing this, had already leapt forward wildly, and took hold of the madwoman, dragging her out of the garden, still continually crying 'Not I, not I, it is he! it is he!' and howling with laughter.

'Stay! that poor woman is my mother!' shouted the Gypsy, in direst grief, summoning up all his strength and rushing after them, and 'My mother! my mother!' repeated the rocks in a landscape still illuminated with the lightning.

All this had happened before the lightning ceased; but now deep darkness descended again; heavy raindrops began to fall from the black clouds, and the distant rocks were still answering, 'My mother! my mother!' in a dark echo.

8

'May the dead rest in peace! her departed soul
rests in the dreams of the angels; do not wake her –
it was ill to her in the world; why should she return? – – –'

LUCJAN SIEMIEŃSKI
The Shadow of Queen Barbara, A Romance of the Year 1551 (1834)

'Open up – – –!' they called from the court.

LUCJAN SIEMIEŃSKI
The Shadow of Queen Barbara

BÁRTA, LYING ON THE GRASS, had meanwhile fallen asleep, repeating disjointed words about the Rhine; as he was turning over uncomfortably, two or three drops of rain fell on his face. Woken by them, and rising to his feet after considerable exertion, he began to reach out in all directions, to fathom where he was. Coming into contact with the table, he traversed its stone surface with his hand, and feeling the glass, began to clink it on the table. No one came; – the silence was long and empty, the night deep. He tottered to one side, consoling himself with his memories: 'It was better on the Rhine, on the Rhine – as soon as I rang, they came straight away!' – A flash of lightning was seen, but only faintly.

In that lightning he caught sight of Leah's white dress in its accustomed place in front of the cottage, and tottered over to her in the porch. He had the glass in his hand, wishing, no doubt, to ask her to fill it for him again, and clutched at her, asking for his drink. – She remained motionless, and did not answer. 'Are you getting up or not? – Leah! you know I come here every day – aye, aye – yes, every day, just for your sake; – on my word; – when I was on the Rhine –'

Again there was an enormous flash of lightning, and the whole landscape was lit up. He suddenly realized that Leah's countenance was lifeless. Her pale face, consumed with grief, stared out gruesomely in the azure lightning. Her eyes were dark, extinguished in death, one staring fixedly into the infinite distance, the other half closed; her teeth were clenched, her lips were half open, and her locks fell chaotically, like a black veil, around her face. Great drops of rain, or of the sweat of her mortal agony, rested on her lifeless brow – on her entire face.

Darkness fell again. Overcome with horror, the veteran began to shout desperately, and, staggering, he dashed out of the garden as quickly as he was able. Then he fell silent – and even the echo from the distant rocks also fell silent. There came a loud clap of thunder; its terrifying crash resounded through the valley, and the rocks continued to answer at length; then a faint rumble of thunder echoed again from the distance, followed by a long, bleak silence. Deep was the night. Now the gale carried over the valley the tolling of great bells; no doubt, they were ringing in the neighbouring villages and in the town to warn of the storm. Mournful were the voices of the distant bells.

Awakened from dreadful dreams by the terrified shouting, the old Jew rushed out of the cottage, though he was perilously ill, and he was followed by the girl, carrying a lighted candle. Its light shed a ruddy glow on Leah's pale face as they reached the porch, and exposed the reason for the veteran's horror. The howling gale extinguished the light; 'I – I have sold – I have destroyed my daughter!' cried out the old Jew, collapsing at her feet.

Now flashes of lightning followed in quick succession, and the rock walls repeated his 'my daughter, my daughter!' together with the thunder. Drops of rain began to fall, thicker and faster, in great globules, until the whole sky exploded into an enormous cloudburst. Against the continuous lightning, the castle bell clanged loudly, without a pause, as if entreating for help, and the bells of neighbourhood churches tolled from the distance, warning of the storm. –

Terrible was the night, but yet more terrible than the night was what had been perpetrated under the darkness of its covering. With brief pauses, the castle bell had tolled through the nocturnal darkness, it had tolled through the savage storm, it had tolled through the teeming rain, and now its clangour was still resounding through a landscape that, as if dismayed by the storm that had passed over it, was reduced to deep muteness and silence. It was now about three o'clock in the morning. Many candles were set up in the office in the castle, and all the officials had gathered there. One after another, they took turns at the castle bell, for the whole establishment had been sent out to search for their lord in case he had lost his way in the storm. – As was his custom, Valdemar Lomecký had ridden to the nearby town towards evening, to visit his acquaintances. Each time he usually returned when nine o'clock had struck; and today it had been past ten, midnight had come, and still he had not returned. Now his faithful retainers were waiting for him vainly. They were convinced that he had lost his way in the storm; for they knew he was unable to sleep peacefully anywhere except in his own castle, in securely locked chambers; they knew he believed that if he were to spend only one single night without sleeping in his own castle, he would surely die that same night. For that reason, the sound of the castle bell continued to be heard without ceasing in the neighbouring forests, so that if he were lost, he could find the way back to his castle following its tolling.

After midnight had passed, in their anxiety they had sent out the last of the servants, to enquire in the nearby town whether the gathering storm had delayed the return of their master, and if he was there, that they should accompany him back to the castle. But three hours had passed since midnight, and no one had returned. The continuous tolling of the bell was still faithfully, but vainly, calling him back into the safety of the castle walls.

It was now three o'clock, and there came a loud knocking on the castle gate. The chief clerk hurried down the steps, followed by a crowd of others, all carrying lights.

They opened the gate, and Judith, the Jews' serving girl, flung herself at their feet, wringing her hands and weeping. They took her into one of the chambers, where she disclosed the news that her ailing master, the old Jew, had just then expired of grief at the death of his daughter; and that she had been so distraught by being left alone that, hearing the sound of the bells and seeing the lights in the castle, she had hastened to give them the news. She also recounted how Bárta, the Gypsies, and the madwoman had remained for some time in the garden in front of their cottage, and that on one occasion, coming out of the cottage, she had overheard the young Gypsy swearing sanguinary revenge on someone. What had happened after that she did not know, because, called by her ailing master, she had been obliged to return into the cottage. A deep silence greeted her account. Horrified, all of them sat averting their eyes, from all corners of the chamber. The candles burned down, one by one, and went out, and, fatigued by the long vigil and its anxieties, one by one they all dozed off. Only the Jews' serving girl remained awake, mourning the deaths of her master and his daughter. The castle bell was silent.

Half an hour passed, and it was now half past three; but there was still deep darkness outside, under a gloomy sky. It was dark in the castle also, now that all the candles had gone out. A deafening hammering at the castle gate was now heard through the castle, and someone outside called in terror: 'For God's sake! Open the gate, open it quickly!' All of them roused themselves, each of them seized with fear, and in the darkness they crowded to the gate.

They opened the gate, and Bárta, without his sabre, and without his hat, which he had lost for a second time, pressed himself urgently upon them. 'For God's sake, lock the gate, lock it! quick, lock it!'

In haste they locked the gate again, and took the trembling Bárta by the hand, leading him upstairs into the chamber.

Candles were lit once more, and 'What has happened? what is it?' they asked the terrified veteran. 'What is it? what has happened?' he began. In his terror he was speaking in a wholly distorted voice, his eyes were popping, and his drenched hair was standing on end. 'What is it? he's there! speared right through; he's there, completely gone – he's been killed there!' – 'Tell us! What do you know?' – they all demanded. 'What do I know?' replied the veteran, 'Oh, yes, I know, I know it all, very well indeed; on my word, all of it!'

'My master! my poor master is dead!' wept Judith. 'What? Good Lord! Judith!' cried Bárta, 'is the old Jew dead? That's impossible!' – 'Yes, yes!' moaned Judith. The officials saw that nothing was to be discovered from Bárta along these lines, and so asked him again directly: 'What do you know? Tell us! Have you seen my lord?' 'My lord? – I've seen him – I've seen him,' replied Bárta, shuddering once more with horror, 'I saw him – and how – he's completely – completely speared right through, completely, right through, killed there!' – 'What! where? Tell us!' came the questions from all sides. 'I was – h'm – I was –,' he mumbled. 'Where were you?' asked the official. 'H'm – I was visiting – hereabouts' – went on Bárta, gesturing at Judith – 'h'm – the late lamented Jew hereabouts', and unable to control his confusion, he began to babble in his customary manner: 'I'm going along and going through the forest, not thinking about anything, and I go on and on through the forest, and I don't know how I got there. And now, I'm going along and not thinking about anything, and suddenly the devil himself pops up here in my path – yes, the devil himself – forgive me – the devil himself – and mutters something about vengeance –' 'But where did you see my lord?' they all asked. 'Right away, I'll tell you!' replied the veteran, and now he related everything he had seen – and indeed rather more than that – interweaving his story with disjointed 'aye, ayes' and 'be damneds'. Its contents were as follows.

9

And in the whole realm of slumbering nature
I slept not, the wind slept not, nor the stars, nor the clouds!

STEFAN GARCZYŃSKI
Autumn Night (1832)

O walls, my walls!
Why are you turning black,
you walls that do not hold his lordship?
They have killed his lordship.

K. W. WÓJCICKI
Jazdów (1834)

… from the tomb they dig out
the corpse, they draw it out by its head and shoulders,
covered with clay and mould;
and it stares out: its face is blue, like pus,
and its body glows in its shroud as if in gold,
its wounds cannot be seen…

JÓZEF DUNIN-BORKOWSKI
The Funeral of the Bey (1834)

EMERGING FROM the little garden in his drunken state, fright-
ened by the thunder and lightning, and also terror-struck by
the spectacles he had witnessed, Bárta missed the path he took
every day. Instead of turning right into the valley, he went left,
below the ruined castle, going up higher and higher through the

rocks and the dense undergrowth, and arriving eventually on the narrow footpath in the dense pine forest above the valley. There was an avenue, thickly seeded with young larch trees, on either side of the footpath; however, the path continued, even and unbroken, far into the forest, and Bárta was prevented from leaving it either to the right or to the left, even though he was staggering from one side of it to the other. He fell repeatedly to the ground, which was thickly covered with deep, soft pine needles; but hearing the incessant ringing of the bell behind him, he rose quickly to his feet each time and staggered on. – The thunder continued to echo through the forest; the wind howled dismally through the thicket, and branches cracked and were snapped off on the forest path. 'Strange – aye – aye –,' he began, 'it's odd – aye, aye, it's impossible; what? h'm – h'm!' Again there was a brilliant flash of lightning; he lowered his head and hurried on. A human form dashed across his path, sobbing, 'My beloved – he seduced my beloved – revenge! – revenge!' – and disappeared in the thicket beside the path; it was followed by the madwoman Angelina, who flashed by across the path, howling with laughter, and then she was gone in the same thicket.

Terrified, Bárta staggered on, and droplets of rain rustled profusely above him in the swaying trees. He continued to wander along this path for about an hour, until the rain had died down.

Now he was walking along a deep, wide track; on both sides above it there were small trees, and his feet were becoming caught in the damp sand. Ragged clouds drifted across the sky, and from time to time the full moon loomed, frowning, over the nocturnal landscape. There were still isolated drops rustling as they fell from the surrounding trees. – Now he was forced to proceed more slowly; – he set each foot down in turn more carefully, to avoid becoming stuck in the deep, damp sand. But in vain; – for, soundly drunk, he became trapped several times, and had to recover control by getting up out of the wet sand. Beset by such predicaments, he entertained himself as usual by telling his stories, and went staggering on.

However, the further he went, the narrower the track became, until it had turned into a very confined path between the rock walls. Higher and higher rose the walls, until finally the sky could barely be seen, and intense darkness shrouded the narrow path. – Pausing, he reached out with his hand, and it touched cold, rounded rocks like the skulls of corpses. He quickly withdrew it; – now the moon emerged from a dark cloud, directly above the path, and on the rock walls Bárta saw nothing but corpses' skulls, bones, stunted trees, and the like. He was on the deep path towards the charnel stone. The moon disappeared in the gloomy clouds. – Once more there was darkness.

Horror-struck, he ran on; he tried vainly to shout; – rebuffed by one side of the path he tottered over to the other, and so, from one wall to the other, fearful of touching either of them, he dashed downwards, continually between the terrible walls, to the charnel stone. Almost shocked into sobriety by his horror and fear, he forgot completely about the Rhine and his stories.

After around half an hour of terrified flight, he was standing, without hat and without sabre, by the charnel stone. In his anxiety he could not decide whether to crawl up it or not. Eventually, pulling himself together, he scaled it, in order to reach the footpath to the ancient oak. At that point, he caught the sound of something like muffled laughter on the other side of it. Although horror-struck, he was also encouraged to some degree by the hope of encountering human company. He crawled out cautiously, determined to find out who might be on the other side.

Shaking with terror, he stood on the charnel stone, and through the dense bushes he looked down on the narrow path in the area below him around the ancient oak. A triumphant and jubilant cry rang out through the foliage of the oak, 'Ha, ha, ha! it is he! it is he! it is not I – not I!', and in the gloom of the glowering moon, which was looking on through the branches and the gloomy clouds above the summit of the hill on the opposite side, he saw a figure capering around the oak, clapping its hands. A second figure was digging some kind of pit, and was bent over almost entirely within it, digging yet deeper. The ghastly form of the ancient oak stretched out its misshapen arms far over the pit, and its rotting material glowed blue in the hollow eyes of its countenance.

Now the moon emerged again from the gloomy clouds, and its clear rays illuminated the branches of the ancient oak, and all the surroundings. 'It is he! it is he! it is not I – not I!' exulted the madwoman, Angelina, former innkeeper and housekeeper, dancing around the oak. By the pit lay something wrapped in a cloak. Drawing near, the madwoman delicately raised the cloak – it was the cloak of the young Gypsy. – And this cloak was covering the bloodstained corpse of Valdemar Lomecký, count of Bork, old Bárta's master. In the moonlight, gold braid glittered on its hunting attire. Indeed it was Valdemar Lomecký, or the young Gypsy, for no one else in the neighbourhood wore gold braid on their clothing. It was a miracle that the veteran did not faint away in horror; – reduced to total sobriety, he crawled discreetly back, and hurried quietly home in the deep sand between the walls.

The moon was shining brightly over the cleft in the rocks; the droplets hanging on the walls glistened blue, like flying sparks, in the moonlight, and the stone skulls loomed under the bushes of blossoms and moss garlanding them.

He ran on without pausing; the tempest howled over his head in the rocky valley. The stone skulls and bones were rumbling behind him, under him, before him; their hollow eyes, in which flying insects were nesting, glistened blue, and seemed to be winking at him. Tripping over something as he came out of the cleft, he fell heavily, and getting up, he saw his own hat lying before him on the path. Grasping it, and running on breathlessly, he disappeared into the dense forest. So he hurried, and came running to the castle towards morning, as we have already heard, and there he recounted all that he had seen, ending his tale with the words, 'Yes, yes, he dug a pit for him, a deep pit, right under the old oak by the charnel stone.'

'Torches! quick, torches!' cried the head official.

Torches were lit, and, leaving an old clerk and Judith behind in the castle, they hurried to the place in question with Bárta, taking spades, hoes, and other tools for digging out the pit. Apart from the fact that Bárta absent-mindedly wandered off the path to the Jews' cottage, which was now silent and deserted, they arrived without delay or interruption at the charnel stone under the ancient oak.

Here they lit more torches, and the ruddy glow of these was cast on the ghastly form of the old oak, and over the wide space around it.

Close to the oak, they found traces of blood, and human footprints, and, farther off, moss, hastily laid out, concealing newly turned earth. The head official himself seized a hoe and began to dig, and one of the officials shovelled out the earth. Six torches burned around the heads of those digging. Deep was the silence; only Bárta, shaking with terror, could be heard from time to time mumbling something about the Napoleonic wars and the Rhine. It was not long before the digging revealed a dead body. They lifted it out of the pit and placed it under the ancient oak, and all the torches were brought to light its face. It was the lifeless countenance of Valdemar Lomecký. His eyes were open, his lips tightly closed, his face peaceful. His mortal agony could not have lasted long.

A long dagger of Italian manufacture had been stuck in his breast until now, and the hand that had dealt him this blow must have been adept at murdering in this manner; for he had been killed with a single wound, which had gone straight to the heart. His splendid hunting attire was muddied and bloodstained; its gold braid glittered in the light of the torches. He was dressed in precisely the attire described by the Gypsy to Leah the previous evening, in the very same place, when he had suspected her of trysting with him.

Unfastening his close-fitting clothing, and opening up his shirt, they found a document on his bare chest, speared to his heart with the dagger. They removed the dagger, and a violent rush of blood, mingled with water, flowed out of the wound. At the top of the paper was written, in large script: 'To be opened immediately after my death'. They hastily improvised a stretcher from the branches of the ancient oak, and placing the corpse upon it, carried it in a mournful procession to the castle.

Four officials bore the corpse of Valdemar, the head official and another official preceding them with lighted torches. The other two, after helping them to negotiate the corpse over the charnel stone, armed themselves, and went searching in the vicinity to find the madwoman and pursue the murderer. Bárta, provided with a new sword, unsheathed it and went with them.

In the east, streaks of white were already announcing the dawn of a new day, and their light blended with the glow of the torches, painting red the sandy skulls and bones of the charnel walls through which the path led to the castle. Individual drops of rain were falling heavily from the leaves of the trees in the forest, and from the bushes on the rock walls.

The others had barely stepped aside with the dead body between the rocks beyond the charnel stone, when desolate gloom closed in on the area around the ancient oak, and with the gloom, terror seized the hearts of those left to search for the murderer. The wet foliage of the ancient oak was shaking in the morning breeze, and its white moss – the grey beard of its ghastly countenance – was fluttering in its motion. Its rotting eyes glistened brightly. Trembling, Bárta began: 'What is the point of searching for anyone in the dark? yes – yes – searching? in the dark – aye, aye. If he were standing right next to me and giving me a – yes, a – I wouldn't have any idea where it had come from. On the Rhine, too, we were searching for a spy – on my word – and it was also at night, but we took –'

'Torches?' asked the older clerk.

'No, no, that'd be a lie – not torches!' replied Bárta, 'he'd always have escaped from far away – no, no – that'd be a lie, not from far away, but he'd have run far away, yes, far away, because he'd have seen us coming. But we took a chap along with us, yes, and he knew where he'd be, and he knew the way – aye, aye, yes!'

'Well, we have you with us for that,' said the older clerk, 'you are like a light for us!'

'Yes – light!' agreed Bárta. 'Light is exactly what my teacher at school used to say; I've been a student too – yes, right up to bursary school!' Although the two clerks were grief-stricken, they were unable to suppress their laughter at this. 'Ha, ha, ha!' laughed Bárta with them, 'what? – who would –? now – now – where had I got to? – Oh, yes, in that bursary school – no, I didn't stay in it; because I got to third grade – one, two – three, yes, three – four – third grade – and my late father – yes, father – was very annoyed, that I didn't manage fourth grade, yes – fourth grade, and he pulled me right out of school – yes!'

Both of them laughed, and Bárta went on: 'Yes, he pulled me out, and because I was a fit boy, he sent me off to the army.'

'And was that why you were that light?' asked the younger clerk.

'No, that wasn't why – that'd be a lie; but the teacher at school never called me anything except a Blight, yes, Blight, and I know for a fact that means something like Light.'

'Surely Bright?' suggested the older clerk.

'No – no – Blight – yes, a Blight!' insisted Bárta, 'but he used to say everything to me in German, and I never understood a single word – aye, aye, – now what's odd about that? not a single word!'

Now they were in the dense pine forest, just where the path led uphill towards the small town in the neighbourhood. Suddenly the younger clerk stopped short, and – as if something had occurred to him – halting his companions, asked them to turn back.

'I think we should go back and fill in that pit,' he said, 'it has just occurred to me; – for if the murderer returns and finds the pit open, he will escape all the sooner if he realizes that his crime is known.'

'The torches should have been put out earlier on our march,' replied the older clerk, 'and the disinterment should have been done more discreetly. But, none the less – let us return.' They went back and began filling in the pit. 'I think,' said the younger clerk, 'that the younger Gypsy did it, the one reported by the Jewess to have sworn vengeance on someone; for this murder has been committed out of revenge. If the murderer had also been a robber, he would certainly have removed his lordship's fine clothes first, or at least cut off the gold braid and buttons –; but those – and also the stone on the buckle, fastening the white feather to his hat – were all thrown into the pit. – But why should he have sought revenge?' He shrugged his shoulders and fell silent. They covered the pit, now filled in, with moss as it had been before.

'On my word, it was out of revenge,' swore Bárta, 'I'm a simple man, yes, very simple, but I can guess. It was out of revenge, I would guess, and this young Gypsy had a deft hand, and those wounds were deep – and that devil who flew at me, crossing my path in the forest, and talked about revenge – aye, aye, by the devil that devil was just like that devilish Gypsy, and straight away I – Glory be to the Father –,' began Bárta loudly, with trembling voice, and twirling his moustache in his anxiety, he burst into floods of tears. A tall, dark figure emerged from the forest, coming across the level space to the ancient oak; gold trimmings glittered at its breast, like those worn by the dead nobleman, and its stride was just like his.

Slowly this figure approached, and the closer it came, the shorter it seemed to be. All three of them concealed themselves behind the ancient oak. Now the figure stopped in front of that same oak. It was the young Gypsy. Close-fitting red trousers embroidered with gold, and a blue cloak embellished with gold braid, were his attire. His breast was bare, and his right hand was hidden over his bare breast. He stood in front of the ancient oak in silence, looking down at the ground before him. 'He is not here,' he said, and once more remained motionless. Slowly, the officials surrounded him, with Bárta in the rear. 'Come along with us to the castle!' ordered one of the clerks.

Turning aside, the young Gypsy walked mutely towards the castle; around him were the officials. Bárta followed behind with his sword unsheathed, and, continually grumbling that it was not the sword which he had found so perfect for fencing, he reminisced about the deeds he had done with it during the Napoleonic wars.

10

Eternity is a wheel, the centuries its spokes...
what is our life? A miserable dot in time!
It is vain to attempt to escape from the wheel ...

– –

May we be clocks on a burning tower:
now the fire grows, as it curls through the roof,
it awaits the end, and the stroke of the hour!

ANON.

Verse for New Year's Day (1832)

IT WAS NOW towards morning, and once more the officials were gathered, sitting in the castle office; all were there, apart from those who had been sent in search of the murderer. The chief official was sitting at a low table, and before him lay the paper document found on the breast of the murdered lord, with the inscription: 'To be opened immediately after my death.'

'His lordship is lying in the castle chapel,' began the chief official, 'and therefore I propose, in accordance with his will, that we should read out the document that was discovered with him.'

All were in agreement, and, setting out more candles, he took the document in his hand, and opened the envelope. It was a lengthy document; he glanced through it quickly, and then began to read:

Valdemar Lomecký, count of Bork, to all who shall read this letter, or who shall have it read to them, greeting; this is my last will and testament. That this document may gain credence, I consider myself obliged to set out matters which I have kept concealed during my lifetime, even though I have been well aware that my inferiors have made conjectures about them all. I do not wish to be lightly judged, nor do I wish my behaviour to be criticized according to circumstances. I have erred; let this public confession be a punishment for my guilt, and perhaps also an instrument of my own revenge, for I am convinced that I shall die at the hand of my own son. –

It was late one evening – about six months after my return from a journey to Italy –, that I was sitting on a rock in front of an arbour in the castle garden, with my pregnant wife Emma, and was suspecting her of unfaithfulness. I was myself unfaithful – why should I not admit my guilt? – When this document is opened and read, my death will already have put an end to my misdemeanours, and the grave will have cancelled the guilty acts I have committed. I was myself unfaithful; and perhaps it is for that very reason that I entertained those suspicions; perhaps they were mere fantasies; to this day I am still unsure. – Because the circumstances may have led to consequences later described, and because I wish to demonstrate the innocence of my wife, I consider myself obliged to describe all the circumstances fully and faithfully. – Deep in thought, I was gazing at the distant mountains, out of which dense vapours were rolling, seemingly at one with the darkened skies. In the distance a storm was raging. Emma sat beside me. I do not know how long we lingered there without exchanging words; I was merely contemplating the inexorable approach of the nocturnal storm, until finally the mountains were so completely hidden under their gloomy vesture that it was as if a single cloud were displayed in them, stretching from the dark earth up to the even darker sky; – and yet neither of us had the confidence to warn the other to leave. The darkness was already profound, and the tempest was raging dolefully in the branches of the trees above us, when Emma, sitting beside me, could no longer bear this silence, so full of horror. 'Do you harbour a suspicion that I have not remained faithful to you as I promised you I would be before the altar of Almighty God?' – I did not answer. – 'Do you imagine that the child I am carrying is the fruit of a sinful liaison with a former friend of yours?' – I remained silent. – 'By the living God I adjure you, tell me on what presumption you base your suspicions, so that I may justify myself in your eyes!' – I still said nothing; those words kindled terrible imaginings in my mind. Provoked to the highest degree of despair by my silence, she rose to her feet, raised her right hand to the gloomy sky and stood before me extending it, as if a ghost from the grave were abandoning its horrific bed and coming to proclaim a dire prophecy. –

The tempest blew about her white vesture, and the storm tore far asunder the dreadful oath of her lips: 'Hear then my oath, since I have never neglected your honour, nor my own! – May the fruit of my womb be misshapen, as abhorrent to human gaze as this night, may it be my ruin and that of all I have ever held dear, and may the hour of its birth be my final hour on earth, if I have sworn this oath to you falsely!'

'May it be my own ruin, if I have defamed you unjustly!' I cried, firmly assured, as I thought, of the truth of my suspicions. At that moment there came a mighty flash of lightning, as if the heavens had opened up, and, in its blinding light, all the mountains, even the most distant ones, came into view, like black waves; then black night closed in once more, and now the invisible mountains repeated, a thousand-fold, the tumult of the terrible claps of thunder. A loud sigh resounded between us, coming from unknown lips, as if it had emerged from her body. –

Five months passed after that night, and the eyes of my wife, after seeing the misshapen fruit of her womb, were now closed in death and saw nothing more. It was a son; – his right hand was slightly larger than his left hand, and his whole body was bent over to one side. His body had red markings, and in the middle of his breast there was a blood-red birthmark resembling hands raised to swear an oath. – Terror seized me when I first saw this mark; and a fear never previously known – a fear of this infant – entered into my heart.

His mother was returned to the earth which had given birth to her; – but I was unable to abide having her son near me. Just at the same time, Angelina – housekeeper in the village, who had been seduced by me in Italy and followed me here – bore a stillborn son – perhaps another son of mine; and in recompense, the son with the birthmark was passed off as hers without her knowledge. Subsequently she always looked after him as her own, and after the deaths of those responsible, no one doubted this. – Living in the ancestral castle was dreadful to me; terrible memories continually provoked the thought of impending vengeance. I went off to the army, anticipating that I would find in battle, if not serenity, at least time to forget past events. It was in vain. – Four years later I returned once more to my desolate homeland, and again the earlier fear took hold of me at the first sight of my housekeeper and my son with the birthmark. He had to depart from my sight. No recourse was available except to send the housekeeper away altogether, giving her substantial compensation. She disdained it. – I wrote informing her that I was unable to live in the vicinity of her son. She believed this, but for reasons other than the real ones. I entreated her, ordered her, to move away from my neighbourhood. It is possible that maternal love cannot be obtained under false pretences, or deceived, – for Angelina did not love her *stepson, even though she was unaware that he was not her own; and she sent him away, declaring that she did not wish to be anywhere save close to me.*

Now with nothing to fear, I received her in my castle; my son had been removed. Although I do not know where he is now, although no one but myself, the writer of this document, knows of these events, nevertheless I believe firmly that when he returns one day, he will be the cause of my death. – He will be recognized by the birth-mark on his breast and by the unequal length of his right hand, as also by his posture, bent over to one side. And even if he himself becomes my murderer, I shall absolve him, and I am convinced that, impelled by his mother's oath or mine, he will involuntarily procure my death.

So the chief official read the whole document; the appalled officials listened attentively. Several times he paused during the reading, and now he concluded, reading the end of the document, with the following words:

By the authority of this document, I ask for forgiveness for him; and my final will is that he, duly recognized, should become the sole heir of my estates. For this reason I have written –

Just then, the doors flew open, and the young Gypsy was standing among them. His attire was muddied and torn; his right hand was concealed in his breast. His face was ashen, and his dark blue eyes were overflowing with sorrow. The officials holding him, and Bárta, followed him into the office. Puzzled, the chief official laid down the document, now almost read through.

'On my word, your Excellency!' said Bárta, sheathing his sword, 'this is certainly the man who killed his lordship.'

The older clerk recounted how they had found him.

'Are you the murderer of Valdemar Lomecký, count of Bork?' asked the chief official, hurriedly rising to his feet.

The Gypsy trembled, but made no reply.

'Suspicion falls entirely upon you; on whom did you swear revenge?' asked the chief official.

The Gypsy remained silent.

They began to question him; the clerk had paper ready, to record his answers.

It was in vain; the Gypsy did not utter a single word. 'We shall get you to speak, all the same,' began the chief official, and ordered him to be brought before the corpse of the murdered lord in the chapel. –

11

*Today ... where there was joy and singing,
now naught but silence.*

Julian Ursyn Niemcewicz
Lamentations of an Exile (1833)

IT WAS ALREADY nearly eight o'clock, but light had scarcely yet dawned on the surrounding landscape; for the whole sky was still overcast, and heavy rain was once more falling on the fields and the wooded mountains. Thick mist was rolling in from the forests, and the neighbouring villages could not be seen at all. A group of men was proceeding downhill through the dense pine forest into the valley described at the beginning of this tale, engaged in lively conversation about the previous night. They were protected from the rain by their broad hats and their black cloaks or old-fashioned jackets, and each time they came to rocky ground, the clatter of their wooden clogs resounded through the deep pine forest.

'What a night that was! On my word, we haven't had thunder like that in years,' said the village JP, hurrying at the head of the group, 'yes, I'm already over fifty, and on my word I've never heard anything like that.'

'Nor have I, nor have I!' chorused the group.

'It was in – yes, five years ago,' said one of them, 'when the church tower caught fire in Lhotec, that it was bad too, but there's seldom been anything like yesterday's storm. Our windows shook so hard that I thought the glass might fall out at any moment.'

'So did ours,' responded the group. – 'It stripped some of the thatch off my barn,' added one of them.

'And the downpour flooded all the equipment in my yard,' said yet another; 'praise be to God that we've weathered it.'

At this point, two forest paths merged into one, and they met some men on the second path.

'Greetings in the name of the Lord!' exclaimed the newcomers.

'Greetings!' replied the others.

'Where are you rushing off to?' they asked.

'Into town,' came the answer. 'With this rain we can't think of working in the fields; so we are going to town to buy provisions.'

'And so are we,' said the others. 'Let us go together.'

'Very well!' and again they recounted how the storm had devastated their village. 'Around midnight it died down a little,' added one of the newcomers, 'and I came out of the cottage, but somewhere there was a bell still ringing continually to warn of the storm. I could not decide whether it was at Smilkov, for the wind was carrying the sound away from the town. Around four o'clock it started raining again, and it seems it won't stop even today.' The brief echo of his voice resounded more hollowly than before in the pine forest; and shortly thereafter they entered the dale, coming into the space around the charnel stone.

As usual, the madwoman was seated under the ancient oak, begging, and she greeted the newcomers with screams of 'It is he, it is he! not I! I am hungry; I am a beggar-woman; it is the moon – O, I know – do not leave me in the rain, hungry!' – One of them opened the bag he was carrying on a stick over his shoulder, and taking out a piece of rye bread, gave it to her; some others followed his example, and soon the madwoman had several pieces in her lap. She immediately began to eat them greedily. They went on, and once more she was left alone in the hollow of the old oak.

'How long has the madwoman been begging here?' asked the JP.

'I really cannot remember how long: I think less than a year,' answered one of them.

'She sits here every day,' said the JP, 'rain or shine – she is always here. Whenever I go to the office on business, I bring her something. – A very good morning to you, Jakub!' he said, greeting the castle porter, who had joined him, coming from the other side with a group of peasants, and now taking the same path through the dale. 'Where have you come from so early?'

'You mean you don't know?' answered Jakub. An imposing old man, he was wearing a cap of black Manchester cotton inlaid with black lambskin, perched over his right ear, a short, tight-fitting jacket, and short lambskin trousers. His long boots were entirely spattered with mud, and the long stick which was supporting him as he was hurrying, with difficulty, was also completely muddied.

'How should I know?' said the JP. 'And you're going out with so many of your neighbours?' –

'So you know nothing?' answered Jakub.

'Nothing at all!' said the JP.

'Nothing about what has happened at the castle?' asked the porter.

'Whatever has happened?' asked the JP.

'Tell him! tell him!' cried the crowd.

'His lordship has become lost!' said Jakub. 'Didn't you hear the bell ringing during the night?'

'I heard it,' said one of them, 'but I thought it was a warning about the storm.'

'Heaven forbid – we were ringing for his lordship,' said Jakub, moving his cap from his right ear to his left ear; 'we were ringing for his lordship, in case he had lost his way, so that he could follow the sound. Now we have been in town, and he is not there either; and now we don't know what to do.'

As they were talking, they passed below the Jews' cottage. 'Why not stop here for some breakfast, Jakub?' suggested the JP.

'Let's do so,' agreed Jakub. 'We shall be losing time,' countered some of them. 'No, friends, let's stop – we can have a quick drink without even sitting down,' said others, and all of them pressed forward, up to the cottage. On the other side of the valley, up the hill, could be seen the men and the servants, who had been sent out to search for his lordship, now returning along the footpaths above the valley.

'We won't be able to get into the room,' laughed Jakub, looking at the group, which now numbered more than twenty men.

'No, we won't!' agreed the JP. 'Let's stay out in the rain – in any case, we shall soon be on our way again. You go, Tobiáš, go and ring the bell!' – and Tobiáš went into the cottage. After a short time he emerged, quite horrified. 'You cannot imagine what has happened! Come and look, the Jew is dead, his daughter also –,' he cried to the others. All of them crowded into the cottage, and those who could not get in pressed up to the window.

Leah was lying dead under the window, on the floor of the room. Her hands were crossed over her breast, her eyes were closed, and her white robe, drenched through, was sprinkled with leaves and blossoms blown in through the broken window by the storm. Her black locks – no longer covered by her turban, which lay unwound beside her – clung, wet through, to her lifeless white brow, her shoulders, her neck and her white robe.

On the bed opposite lay the old Jew, her father, also dead; he was wearing the same attire as that he had worn when the Gypsies first arrived there. Tools, pewter vessels, and lamps, scattered by the storm wind, lay about the room. All of them stared, appalled, at the desolate scene, unable to utter a word. And at that moment, a tall man in a tattered jacket, with a large lambskin cap drawn tight over his ears, rushed in among them. 'Jakub!' he cried, 'go to the castle immediately! Go now! His lordship has been killed! They have brought in the murderer. I'm running to town with the news,' and, pointing at the mud on his boots, which were pulled up over his stockings and fastened with thongs below the knee, he added: 'I must run, never mind the puddles!' Even before finishing what he had to say, he was already off in the distance. Jakub, wholly appalled, dashed back to the castle as quickly as he could.

Shouting to those going along on the other side, all of them hurried after him, and those running on the other side answered, 'We already know!' Many of them took off their clogs so that they could run to the castle more quickly.

The castle courtyard was completely filled with people, both women and men, old and young, in a throng around the chapel, and the veteran Bárta was telling them all he knew. People were continually arriving. Now the porter came, and a great crowd of peasants with him. Everyone pressed forward behind him towards the chapel, but the chapel was locked. Noisy clamour filled the courtyard. Bárta had already told the crowd what he knew at least five times, and he began again as soon as someone new arrived.

All this happened while the chief clerk was reading the document, and while the Gypsy was being brought in and vainly questioned.

Now the doors of the office opened, and the Gypsy was led across the courtyard to the chapel. There was an enormous throng in the courtyard, especially near the chapel door: everyone was anxious to catch a glimpse inside the chapel. However, the officials entering the chapel with the Gypsy locked the doors behind them; Bárta, at the door, was obliged to drive away the press of people with his new sabre, and whiled away his time, and that of the crowd, at some length, by recounting what had happened – while continually inter-weaving similar events from the Napoleonic wars.

The castle chapel was narrow, but long. Its circular windows were curtained on both sides. Above, on a bier before the single altar, lay the murdered Valdemar Lomecký, count of Bork, covered in a black cloth. It was murky outside, and sombre in the chapel, for the dim light penetrating through the curtained windows was barely adequate. A simple cross was raised on the altar, and a white linen cloth was placed to cover it, as if they had only just taken Christ down from the tree of his Passion. On either side of the cross there was a gilded angel in a black veil, kneeling in prayer.

Entering, they locked the doors behind them; the ray of light that had forced its way in through the open doors was extinguished once more, and gloom again shrouded the altar and the bier. The Gypsy made a few quick steps towards the dead body; but, plunging his right hand yet further into his breast, again stood still. The officials remained by the doors. The chief official ordered lights to be brought. Torches were lit, casting their ruddy glow over the tombs of the Lomecký dynasty, counts of Bork, buried here, and tinting the cross and the kneeling angels.

'Are you the murderer of the man whose dead body is now lying here before your eyes?' asked the chief official. The Gypsy gave no answer. The cloth was opened out; – pale, but serene, was the face of Valdemar Lomecký. His elegant hunting clothes were spattered with mud, the pure white feather of the hat lying next to him drooped over his breast, adorned with gold braid, and screened its deep wound. The Gypsy trembled; he made two quick steps nearer, and a warm rush of blood flowed over his right hand, raised above his head, on to his face, turned towards heaven. For the first time he was seeing the face of the man whom he had regarded only as the seducer of his beloved, the man who had entirely destroyed peace and happiness in a breast that was in any case eternally morose.

There was renewed shouting in the courtyard, and knocking on the chapel door, and the servants returned, bringing with them the older Gypsy, whose place of concealment from them in the forest had aroused their suspicions. Arriving at the castle and discovering that the lord had been murdered, they had concluded that he must be the lord's murderer.

Both prisoners were brought into the office. – The face of the older Gypsy was entirely altered. His eyes, his brow, and his whole countenance were distinguished by an uncommon serenity; all the earlier horror had disappeared from his wrinkled brow, and all the passions that had previously competed to display themselves in his face seemed to have been extinguished in his breast. He showed no discontent, no fear. Like the younger Gypsy, he too made no answer to any questions. –

In less than an hour, officials came from the town, sent by the criminal court, to investigate all the circumstances, and some soldiers came with them. Taking note of the wounds of the dead body, and determining the extent of the heritable estate, they returned to town with the prisoners. The chief castle official gave them the document that had been found with the dead body, and followed them with some other officials, in order to give precise details; and Bárta went with the prisoners, telling the soldiers who were guarding them about his adventures in the wars. A great number of villagers from the neighbourhood accompanied them into the town, disregarding the continual persistence of the rain.

12

What further resistance should then be made?
They are striking in the council.

Dominik G. Magnuszewski
Wallachia, A Historical Fragment (1834)

O, for how long a pitiless dream
was tormenting my childhood years!
I sang all through the time of my youth,
plucked flowers in those meadows,
all things were fair and sweet,
for I felt as yet no loss.

Alojzy Skarzyński
My Youth (1829)

IT WAS THREE O'CLOCK in the afternoon. The councillors
and associated judges were met in the courtroom of the nearby
town. The rain had now passed over, and the sun was showing
fitfully through the ragged clouds on the green landscape, also
casting a languid light into the courtroom through its Gothic
windows. It was a large, star-shaped chamber; on each side of
it there were low Gothic arched windows, except that on the
north side there was the single entrance door. A silver cande-
labra hung from the Gothic vaulted ceiling. Above the south
window, opposite the door, there was the coat of arms of the

town, and above the other windows were displayed banners of assorted colours. On the walls around the windows hung shields, armour, and the like. Opposite the door stood a long table covered with a yellow cloth, behind which the councillors took their places in a long line; and set out on it there was a multitude of papers, inkwells, pens, sand shakers, and so forth. The castle officials, also including the chief official, were already present. Three o'clock struck, and the presiding judge entered the chamber. The councillors bowed, he took his seat, and at a signal the bailiffs led the madwoman, Angelina, into the court-room. She had been found near the ancient oak, had quickly been taken prisoner, and had been brought to the nearby town.

Now she came slowly into the centre of the chamber, leaning on a long, heavy stick; the bailiffs remained on either side of the door. She remained standing in the centre, raised her head, and gazed at the distant landscape, motionlessly, through the low window.

Her head was covered with a shawl, and only one or two grey locks coiled over her wrinkled face and her bare neck, gaunt and battered by the misfortunes of time and weather. Above the waist her body was covered only by a rough, ragged shift, and, apart from it, she was wearing nothing but a single red petticoat. Over her shoulder, from right to left, a bag hung by a narrow strap, and in it there were some scraps of dry bread and fruit. At every step her bare, muddy feet left footprints on the white floor. Her whole figure personified obdurate stubbornness.

The clerk made his pen ready, but the first question of the presiding judge, 'Were you at the Jews' cottage yesterday?'

remained unanswered. 'I am asking you,' he repeated, 'whether you were at the Jews' cottage yesterday evening?' The madwoman said nothing. 'Do I have to instruct you how to answer?' he continued. She remained silent and motionless. 'Fetch a bench!' the judge ordered the bailiffs. Falling to her knees, the madwoman cried in a loud voice, 'It is not I, not I, it is he, it is he! Not I, I am a poor woman, a madwoman, a poor beggar-woman; – why do you leave me dying of hunger? Have mercy on my wretchedness, have pity on my naked-ness! Alms! Alms!' The word 'alms!' was cried out in a terrible, exceptionally sonorous voice; after this, in deep silence, she lowered her head. 'Speak!' ordered the presiding judge, 'were you in the Jews' cottage?' 'Not I, not I, it was he! it was he!' replied the madwoman. 'He? Who is "he"?' asked the judge. 'It is he, it is he! he seduced me – he seduced them – all, all of them; not I! it is he, he drove away my child, the dead moon reaches out to him, to him!' and again she fell silent.

The judge saw that nothing was to be achieved in this manner, and began to ask her directly: 'Who murdered Count Valdemar of Bork? You know about this – you were there when the pit was dug!'

Angelina drew herself up erect; her eyes, fixed on the wall, were blazing with a terrible light, and her whole body began to tremble violently, but she gave no answer. The judge made a sign, and the bailiffs led both Gypsies into the chamber. 'Which of these?' asked the judge. The madwoman raised her eyes, and, throwing herself around the neck of the old Gypsy, pointed at the younger, with finger extended, saying, 'It is he! it is he!'

'Are you then the murderer of the Count of Bork?' asked the judge. The younger Gypsy, still concealing his right hand in his breast, stepped forward, but did not utter a word.

'His right hand was bloodstained when I brought him before the count's dead body!' testified the chief castle official.

'Show your right hand!' ordered the judge.

The Gypsy remained immobile.

'Bailiff!' called the judge, waving his hand.

The bailiff went over to the young Gypsy, and tearing his garments open, bared the Gypsy's right hand and his breast.

The Gypsy remained immobile.

His right hand was dug deeply into his breast; blood flowed over it and also over his breast, from its hectic wound.

There was a blood-red birthmark, like hands raised in an oath, in the middle of his breast.

The officials were dumbstruck, and 'Parricide!' echoed, like a single sigh, from every lip through the great chamber.

'That is my son, my son!' cried the madwoman Angelina, looking at his birthmark. Throwing herself around his neck, she pointed at the older Gypsy with outstretched finger, crying, 'It is he! it is he! It is he! Not I, not my son! – my son! my son! it is he, it is he!' – and running from each Gypsy to the other, she was continually crying out meaningless words, until, tired out, she collapsed between the two of them in the middle of the chamber, and, beside herself, remained lying on the floor, still whispering 'My son! my son!'

Stepping forward, and gesturing with his bloodstained hand towards the recumbent Angelina, the younger Gypsy began: 'Yes, this is my mother! Why should I further conceal my birth? My parentage is of no concern to me. – She is my mother! The cottage you call the Jews' cottage was the haven for my cradle, and the high rocks by the old castle were the walls of the home of my childhood. But one night when I was about four years old, my mother took me far – far away. For two days and two nights, we went on walking; on the third night, I drifted into sleep under the trees in my mother's lap – and in the morning I was left alone in a deep forest. No one answered my weeping, my cries; I wandered a whole day, finding no way out. Night fell. Weary and hungry I staggered through a deep dale, and suddenly I see a red glow and, soon after that, a great fire. I come closer. Around the fire lies a motley crowd in strange confusion. A puppy is being suckled at a sow's breast, a piglet at the udder of a bitch. Children and women are lying half naked in the dewy grass, with no covering except their thick tresses. Fearful squalor! – It was a tribe of Gypsies. When I was abandoned, they took me in among themselves, and this man'– gesturing towards the older Gypsy – 'became my father and taught me all I have learned, taught me to read and write.

'For many years I wandered with them, waging a constant battle with wind, weather, and the elements. Six months ago, my father (now my guide) and I separated from their group; we wandered into this region, and a little while ago we came by chance into this valley. Immediately I recognized this region, although I did not disclose this even to my guide. Well-known here since my childhood, I found a cave in the rocks to sleep in, and, in it, this madwoman – ignorant of the fact that she was my mother. I had made enquiries about my mother – in vain. Apart from what the old veteran told me about her as the former landlady at the inn, no one knew anything about her. I fell in love – ah!' – His mournful eyes fell on his bloodied right hand, and he relapsed into deep silence. In his quick unfolding of the events relating to himself, he had put Leah quite out of his mind, but remembering her now in his narrative, he was overcome with enormous grief, with a force hitherto concealed. He wept for the first time since he was four years old; but no tear flowed over his pale face that was not mingled with drops of blood.

'Go on with your story, and about her too,' admonished the judge. 'She is dead now.'

A terrible cry arose from the Gypsy's lips; then he relapsed into deep silence. But after some time, coming to himself, he continued with his account thus: 'Yesterday, for the first time, the madwoman, whom no one knew, admitted that she was the seducer of my mistress, and that she was the former landlady of the inn; and I realized that she was my mother.'

The Gypsy said nothing more; Angelina rose to her feet, as if waking from a deep dream, and as if her lost reason had returned to her, she spoke intelligibly: 'This is my son! my unhappy son! and I am the reason for his unhappiness!'

'And are you the murderer of Count Valdemar of Bork? All the evidence speaks against you!' cried the judge and the chief castle official. – The Gypsy did not answer.

'Here, read this!' ordered the judge, giving him the document obtained from the chief castle official, which had been found beside the murdered count. 'Perhaps this will induce you to acknowledge your terrible guilt!'

As if in a dream, the Gypsy took the document, and opening it out, began to read it out loudly and clearly: 'Valdemar Lomecký, count of Bork, to all who shall read this letter, or who shall have it read to them, greeting; this is my last will and testament.'

So the Gypsy read out the whole document – throughout, as if from deep sleep, without emotion, without variation in his voice –, until he reached the words 'his right hand was slightly larger than his left hand –'. At these words, he began to tremble dreadfully, and read on slowly, in a terrible, deep voice, until, at the words 'He had to depart from my sight!' he involuntarily clenched his bloodied right hand; reading further, 'He will be recognized by the birthmark on his breast and by the unequal length of his right hand, as also by his posture, bent over to one side,' he pressed it, outspread, over the birthmark on his breast there described. For a time he fell silent, sunk in deep thought. Then he lifted his bloodied right hand out and pressed it to a brow that was like cold marble – and the birthmark on his breast was obscured completely under the impress left by his bloodied right hand. More and more quietly, he read: 'And even if he himself becomes my murderer, I shall absolve him, and I am –'

Now he ceased reading. Tightly he gripped the document, and gazed into it with unblinking eyes. He was like a statue, as if turned to stone, the picture of the deepest sorrow that is the precursor of despair.

The older Gypsy remained motionless. The madwoman listened attentively, however. At first she was calm, but, hearing more, she threw herself to the ground, writhing like a worm over the open floor; from time to time she beat her brow, her breast, with clenched fist, but no sound issued from her mouth. At the words 'even if he himself becomes my murderer' – she abruptly pulled herself together, and with raised voice, cried: 'It is not he, not he, he is not my son! he – it is he! – not I, not I – it is he, the murderer of his own father!' She pointed at the younger Gypsy, and, crying 'It is he! it is he!', threw herself on the breast of the older Gypsy.

He pushed her away, however, and moved into the centre of the chamber. His countenance was serene and peaceful; all the earlier horror and passion had disappeared from it, and the flame of vengeance had been extinguished in his eyes as also in his heart. 'This woman is my former mistress!' he said, gesturing to the madwoman, Angelina. 'Yesterday I recognized her when she named herself; and to avenge her upon her seducer, I murdered the father of this youth. This letter here shall bear witness against me!' He took out a rolled document, and handed it to the judges. 'And, when I have been convicted of my crime, let this letter be a keepsake, and, perhaps, a vindication of me for this youth, so that he may not execrate me for the death of his father, he for whom I was more of a father than the man who begot him!'

The judges read the letter aloud; once more they asked the older Gypsy whether matters were as reported in the letter, and how he now pleaded. – 'It is so –,' declared the Gypsy, 'this letter was written long before I recognized her again. I did not think then that it would stand in evidence against me.' He uttered no further words. The silence was profound. The judges made their decision, and their unanimous verdict was this: 'In three days' time you will be hanged by the neck until you are dead!' Beside herself, the madwoman prostrated herself at his feet, and the younger Gypsy stood as before, turned to stone, immobile, like a statue. Tightly he gripped the letter of his murdered father and gazed into it with unblinking eyes. Under his breath he whispered, devoid of memory, oblivious of the sense of the individual words: 'My father! – my father seduced my mother – no, he murdered my mother – by my mother – no, he seduced my mistress by my mother – he seduced the mistress of my father – seduced my mother – and my father murdered my father!'

13

Nick: *Before my long journey*
in my mind I shall return to the abode of my parents.

JULIUSZ SŁOWACKI
Maria Stuart (1830), act IV, scene 4

Hejdenrich: *Hope, then! God has granted me*
the right to give absolution to those who are stained with blood.

JULIUSZ SŁOWACKI
Mindowe (1829), act III, scene 1

THE YOUNG GYPSY was declared innocent, and pronounced to be the young Count Valdemar of Bork; and, in accordance with his father's will, he came into the inheritance of the whole estate. He remained undemonstrative and taciturn, whatever was done with him. Now an announcement was made, in front of the town hall, that the son of the murdered count had been found, and loud cheers from the assembled rabble echoed through the town. Then the bailiffs led out the old Gypsy, announcing that he was the murderer of the count of Bork, and that he was to be hanged in two days' time. The assembled people again cheered loudly.

The same evening, the young Gypsy, now Valdemar, count of Bork, was led out as lord of the castle in a solemn and noisy procession – he who had stood as a Gypsy, as a prisoner, in front of a corpse, not recognizing it as that of his murdered father, that same morning. They rode the length of the deep dale, with two pairs of horses, preceded and followed by a crowd of people crying, 'Long live his lordship!' The chief official, and another official, were seated with young Valdemar in the coach.

He, however, sat with downcast eyes, not lifting his head, and paying no heed to his surroundings. Now they were riding down beyond the stream, close to the lake; above them lay the Jews' cottage, and above that the old castle. At the old castle, on each side of the valley, and also in the Jews' garden, there were crowds of spectators. Hastening ahead, to tell everyone what he knew, Bárta was standing on the stone table in the Jews' garden, narrating the day's events at the top of his voice to the group crowding around him. Now they were riding with the new young count directly below: 'See, that man used to be the young Gypsy, aye, aye – yes – the young Gypsy; – but now he's not a Gypsy, now he's his lordship, young Valdemar Lomecký of Bork, son of his murdered lordship, – aye – aye – so cheer him! Long live his lordship!' cried Bárta. 'Long live his lordship!' came the shout from the whole crowd, and the rocks replied, 'Long live his lordship!'

Young Valdemar was roused from his deep contemplation by the familiar voice of Bárta. Raising his head, he looked up. He recognized the Jews' cottage, and, clasping his hands together, laid them on his ravaged heart, dropping his head deep over his numbed breast. 'Long live his lordship!' was still echoing from the rocks in the distance. The sound of the castle bells and the loud reports of the big guns echoed through the deep dale; – until they rode into the castle.

Young Valdemar locked himself in his chambers, and no one ventured to speak to him or to rouse him from his distressful thoughts. The servants kept watch the whole night at the doors of his apartment. – In the morning, the murdered count was laid to rest in the tomb of his ancestors below the castle chapel. Again there was a throng of people in the castle courtyard, but only the officials and the son of the murdered count were admitted to the chapel. The crowd, pressing to and fro around the open doors, was able to glimpse their murdered lord once more only through them. Bárta and old Jakub guarded the doors. – In the evening, Leah and the old Jew were buried. Some neighbours bore their coffins uphill at sunset to the Jewish cemetery; only Judith and old Bárta went with them.

A bright morning dawned over the mountains. It was the third day, on which the old Gypsy was to be executed. Angelina, the madwoman, was sentenced to accompany him to the place of execution and then to be consigned permanently to a lunatic asylum. – The old Gypsy prepared himself for execution; – he was composed, his face was unchanged since the sentence pronounced on him, but his locks had turned entirely grey in the two previous days. He was pacing with slow step in the long, dark room in the tower of the courthouse. The floor, walls, and ceiling of this room were of dark stone squares; directly opposite the Gothic arch of the entrance was a small window, very narrow inside but somewhat broader outside, the only one in the whole long room. To one side stood a small oak table, and on it a small black cross, with a garland of white and red roses next to it.

Behind the table sat an old monk, preparing the Gypsy for his death. It was seven o'clock; – the execution was to take place at eight.

Young Valdemar, count of Bork, his former companion, came to take his leave of him. The priest left the room, and the two of them were left alone – except for the guard pacing outside the open doors.

They stood facing one another without speaking a word; – old Giacomo gazed beseechingly into the face of young Valdemar, but he fixed his eyes on the stone floor. – They stood facing each other for a long while, and there was deep silence in the long room. – Finally, the old Gypsy stepped forward.

'There is little time now,' he said in a weak voice, 'before this hour passes; I am reconciled with the world, and my act – my crime – will perhaps soon be forgotten as shall I myself. I am justified in my own eyes, and perhaps I shall be justified in your eyes by the letter that was given to you by the court. She, my accomplice in my action, my former mistress, will be punished with me. – She is obliged to witness my death, I am obliged to look upon her as I die; then a dark cell will forever enclose her, and a darker one will hold me.' –

He ceased speaking. The long, dark chamber was silent, and all that could be heard was the noise of the crowd assembling in the distance for the execution of the Gypsy.

'I am also reconciled with her,' continued the Gypsy. 'God, who has seen into my heart, forgives my guilt; you, too, forgive me!'

For the grief in his heart, Valdemar was unable to answer. Again there was silence.

'Do you give no answer? Do you not forgive me?' Silence. From the next room the voice of the madwoman could be heard. 'Not I, not I! It is he, it is he!' she cried, moaning loudly.

'I was a father to you,' said Giacomo, 'when your own father abandoned you; – I was your companion, your friend, when you were still a Gypsy; – am I nothing to you now?'

Again silence; – the dull sound of the drum could be heard below.

'The time is going; – they will come now to take me out of the town; I shall have to go –' Again a deep, long silence. 'Here, see!' cried the Gypsy, and going up to Valdemar, took him to the single window nearby. Faint, Valdemar collapsed next to the window.

Rising to his knees, however, he looked out of the narrow window with its Gothic arch at the broad landscape.

The sun was up over the high mountains, blue in the distance, whose rounded cones provided an edging in a great circle for the distant, fertile plain.

On it, distant fields alternated with woods with young trees and isolated villages. Closer, beyond the town, in the middle of a broad, green meadow, there was a high, rounded, green hill. On it was thronging a countless number of people from the vicinity. On its highest summit, there were two young trees; between them towered a gallows, and around this there were armed guards. Crowds of people were continually thronging the paths from the town to the hill of execution.

'Here!' cried the Gypsy, 'here, see! When an hour has passed, my last sparks of life will be extinguished on that hill; – do not leave me – do not leave me, my gracious lord, do not leave me to depart from this world without your forgiveness.'

At that point the priest entered, and the hangman with him; some soldiers remained outside the doors. Young Valdemar offered the Gypsy his hand, – but could not utter a word.

'Farewell, my lord!' cried the old Gypsy in a loud but trembling voice, 'farewell, and if ever you go south, – greet my Venice!'

Two great tears rolled down his wrinkled face.

'Goodbye, my son, goodbye!' he said, in a weak voice, and left the room. The priest and the hangman followed him.

The doors were closed, and young Valdemar, half beside himself, turned his face to the stone wall – remaining kneeling, alone in the dark room.

The dull thud of a drum could be heard below; then deep silence again followed. Valdemar remained continuously kneeling, as if in a dreadful dream, by the narrow window. After about a quarter of an hour, he was roused by a loud din. A long procession could be seen through the window, making its way across the meadow beyond the town. In two lines stood a crowd who had come from the town and also from further away. Among them were some soldiers, going ahead of the procession, to the dull sound of a drum draped in black; two lines of horsemen had also come. Surrounded by a large company of soldiers, old Giacomo walked with slow but firm step behind them, carrying in his hand the small cross, and the garland of white and red roses. The priest was on one side of him, the hangman on the other. He was followed by two henchmen, leading the madwoman, Angelina, tied on a long rope. Leaping into the air, even turning somersaults, and running to and fro, she was crying, 'It is not I, not I! it is he, it is he! – my curse! my child in the hand of the moon!' – and, from time to time, singing strange songs in a high, rasping voice. – It was a fearful sight. – Another two lines of horsemen followed, and some soldiers completed this terrible procession. Once more, Valdemar collapsed on the cold stone floor of the dark room.

Thus the procession reached the summit of the hill of execution. The horsemen remained below, with their flashing broadswords dispersing the crowd that was pressing on to the hill. The company above parted, and the old Gypsy mounted the gallows. His face was pale, or, rather, grey, in colour. With the priest he recited the Lord's Prayer. After the prayer was completed, he stood, according to the custom of that place, before the judge, pleading for mercy.

'God is merciful!' replied the judge.

The countenance of the Gypsy blushed a deep purple, and again went pale; and once more a red blush alternated with pallor in his countenance.

He pleaded a second time, and the judge again replied, 'God is merciful!'; he pleaded a third time, and the answer was the same.

The veins on the Gypsy's forehead stood far out, every limb of his trembled, and his face was as pale as death. Under his breath, he prayed the Lord's Prayer once more with the priest. Everyone had their eyes turned up towards him, and there was deep silence among the enormous crowd. The hangman threw the noose around the neck of the criminal, and bared his breast. Every hair on the head of the Gypsy stood on end, his beard bristled, and his eyes protruded prominently. The veins on his forehead stood far out, and great drops of sweat fell from his pale brow. –

A loud sigh went up from the crowd, and the unfortunate man swung from the high pin. A terrible shriek went up from below – no human tongue can express it – and the madwoman collapsed below the support of the gallows.

They lifted her up, and removed her to the lunatic asylum.

Her punishment was the most terrible of all, although the most merited. From that time she had not a moment of peace, constantly seeing before her the execution of her lover, whom she had earlier abandoned and deceived, leading him to a desperate act, and therefore to a shameful death; finally, in desperation, breaking her shackles, she tore her veins open with her teeth, and in that manner she put a horrifying end to a horrifying life.

14

'I shall take you to a distant land,
where our love will not be censured.
You shall be my wife, my betrothed,
I shall be faithful to you eternally.'

AUGUSTYN BIELOWSKI
Nastia (1834)

Alone among so many, I wander the world,
perhaps a stranger's hand will close my eyelids in my last hour;
ah, brethren, if you do not feel how the homeland is yours,
you will leave it for a while, and then you will feel affection for it.

STEFAN GARCZYŃSKI
The History of Wacław (1832)

THUS THE GYPSY was displayed on the raised gallows until evening; around him were the guards and a crowd of onlookers, below him a cloth was spread out, and on it were two drops of blood and some small coins.

The letter acknowledging his guilt, which he had given to the judges, and which had been passed to the younger Gypsy, read thus:

When the cold earth receives an unhappy man into her womb, granting him the peace he has sought in vain on earth, this letter will explain my circumstances and justify my revenge, if I achieve the goal I have long sought.

I am not a Gypsy by birth; I am from Italy, born in Mestre, and Venice is my home. – I was a gondolier. When I was about twenty years old, I fell in love with a Venetian girl, and I swung contentedly in my boat below the Rialto Bridge. I had my stand there, and my girl was always there with me. One day – it was a Sunday morning – my mistress came to me. 'Giacomo!' she said, in a loving voice, 'Giacomo, I must visit my aunt in Mestre, to give her some gifts from my parents; I shall receive some wine and some walnuts from her in return. You must take me there; we shall return before noon!'

I was all the more ready to do this, as some of the young men from the city were asking to be taken to Mestre. My colleague took his position at the prow of the boat; I took mine at the stern. – After a time we were in the lagoons, and soon Venice was behind us, bathed in the waters encircling her.

We sailed to Mestre, and at the harbour there was a swarm of people, because a foreigner had come to town. Crowding on the square, the local inhabitants were chattering about a variety of things; but, seeing the carriage, they surrounded the newcomer, as is usual there.

The gondoliers argued noisily which of them was to take the foreigner to Venice. He was a slender young man; his fine clothing showed him to be a wealthy youth. He spoke excellent Italian. I also joined the gondoliers, and spoke to him, asking him whether I could take him in my boat. Looking at me, he promised me that he would sail to Venice with me. I immediately asked my mistress to conclude her business quickly, before the belongings of the foreigner were trans-ferred from the coach to the boat. She ran off; soon she returned, but she brought nothing with her, saying that she had not found her aunt at home. The things that belonged to her had been left in the apart-ment, and now she would return with us. After a time we boarded the boat. The foreigner and both of his servants were inside the cabin, and my mistress stayed out on deck with me. My colleague and I, expecting a handsome reward, rowed strongly, and after a quarter of an hour we had passed the canal and were in the lagoons. The foreigner came out to us. He had meanwhile changed his clothing. Close-fitting yellow trousers, long boots, and a richly braided green jacket were his attire. His throat was uncovered, except for a white collar fastened closely around his neck. On his head he had a hat adorned with a white feather. He was a handsome man – I still see him before me today, and the memory of it –; but – no, what I feel – but I wished to write a letter to justify myself, and so I continue –

– he was a handsome man. Even in Mestre, I was apprehensive of telling him to come with me, considering that my mistress was sailing with us.

Greed for gain overcame the beginnings of jealousy; now I have had to pay dearly for this. – It was now nearly eleven o'clock; the sun was almost directly overhead. In front of us rose the towers and palaces of Venice, out of the waters encircling her, and the peal of bells drifted over the surface of the waters.

The foreigner was conversing with my mistress, asking her about access to towers, palaces, and so forth. She was answering his questions. I was trembling. We progressed as far as the Grand Canal; the foreigner disembarked, ordering his servants to take his belongings to the Hotel Grande Bretagne, and my colleague offered to show them the way. He himself wished to see the city, and asked my mistress to take him to the Piazza San Marco. I wanted to take him there in the boat, explaining that he would see many noteworthy palazzi on the way. But he insisted. He promised a large sum, for the trip from Mestre, and also for her service as his guide. I wanted to take him *myself alone, or go with them; but my colleague had left with his servants, and the boat could not be left unattended. She also wanted to go with him, saying that she was obliged, in any case, to visit her parents on some business.*

My jealousy increased, though I did not wish to admit to it; but to prevent this being obvious in front of the foreigner, I pretended I had told her where to go. Meanwhile, I was considering how large the fee might be for her service as a guide. – She laughed at my jealousy, and, circumventing her reproof, I told her she was avaricious. She said, however, that the money she would receive would be mine, and greed for gain once more overcame my jealousy; – I consented, and soon the foreigner disappeared with my mistress, in a narrow street behind the Rialto Bridge.

No sooner had they left than a storm began to rage in my breast. Several times I wanted to abandon the boat and rush after them. Several times I stepped on to dry ground from the boat, only to climb back into the boat. Once I got as far as the Rialto Bridge, before returning again to the boat. Again I mounted the Rialto Bridge, ran across it, and finally seeing my colleague coming, I beckoned to him to come to the boat, and I hastened to the Piazza San Marco.

It was almost noon. There were crowds of people surging out of the basilica of San Marco. Crowds everywhere – in front of the church, down to the quay, and right up to the palace opposite. I ran about everywhere. Several times I asked about my mistress, among acquaintances who were going about the crowd with fruit. – No one had seen her. I ran about the Ducal Palace; I was down at the quay – among the fruit sellers – in Napoleon's Giardini; she was nowhere. I ran to her house. She had not yet arrived. I hastened to the Hotel Grande Bretagne. I asked. The foreigner was already in his rooms in

127

the hotel. No one knew, however, whether any woman had come with him. I wanted to burst into his rooms; but, recovering myself, I went back to her apartment. She had now returned home.

In such passages in the letter it could be seen how his memory had affected the old Gypsy. His trembling hand was evidence of suppressed rage and blazing jealousy, and the style, too, betrayed jealous haste. It was also clear that some gap had interrupted his writing here, and that the narration had been continued, possibly some days later, as follows:

She was at home; she said I should go away for a short time when she had returned home. She gave me money that she had obtained from the foreigner, for showing him around the basilica of San Marco, and for showing him the way to his hotel. It was a considerable sum, and yet I supposed that she had not given me all the money she had obtained; why I thought that – I did not know myself. On the surface I was content, but mistrust boiled within me.

One evening I sailed with some foreigners to the Lido. The sun had set behind Venice, and long red streaks stretched out in the sky and over the surface of the water. A second boat was sailing opposite us, and singing and playing could be heard from the open entrance to its cabin. It seemed to me that I saw the foreigner I had taken to Venice from Mestre there, and the figure of a woman was with him in that boat. – Could it be my mistress? – A deep sense of pain almost shattered my breast. I rowed more slowly, but, as I approached that boat more closely, they closed the door of its cabin. A strange man was standing at the helm. I wanted to see into the cabin of the other boat, and called desperately, asking him to open the cabin curtains; but the stranger laughed at me, they passed us, and I had seen nothing. – I rowed east – I was obliged to do so – and their boat sailed west towards Venice. – Hot tears flowed down my cheeks, and I watched them until they disappeared in the canal between the Ducal Palace and the prison below the Bridge of Sighs.

I sat at the Lido alone, gazing towards the east as the full moon was just rising from the dark ocean. I whispered words without meaning, oaths without purpose, to the moon rising beyond the sea. The silver waves were mirrored on the dark shore.

After about an hour we sailed back to Venice. The foreigners alighted at the Dogana, and I sailed to my stand. I entered the canal between the Ducal Palace and the prison below the Bridge of Sighs, without knowing why. – The moonlight fell in a long shaft on the narrow canal, and on the high walls above me. I sang, and I wept; I did not know what, or why. Mooring my boat, I stepped out on dry ground. The thought troubled me: 'Why did she not come to me in the afternoon? She was with me in the morning; why did she not come in the afternoon? – She scarcely ever comes to me in the afternoon. – But why did she not come today?' These and similar objections mounted up within me. Finally, unable to wait any longer, I hastened to her lodging. She was at home. It seemed to me more orderly than at other times; it was late when we took our leave from each other. I reproached her; she wept, saying that I did not believe her. I trusted her again, but not completely. I went and spent the whole night in my boat, on the open sea beyond the Lido. The following day, I went to her apartment in the afternoon, to make sure that she was at home. – From that side, from Napoleon's Giardini, was coming the foreigner, whom I hated so much. The fearful storm within me grew stronger. I hastened, indeed I ran, to her lodgings. Her family were all standing in front of the house. Abruptly I asked whether she was at home. They said she was. I went into the room.

The table was littered with her hairpins, handkerchiefs, and so forth. She was lying on the bed. She was asleep, or feigning sleep. I roused her, and, fixing her with an impassioned gaze, I asked her whether anyone had been there. – No one, she said. I asked more urgently. Again she wept, saying that I did not believe her.

I ran off; a fearful flame of blazing jealousy was burning in me. I spent the night on the terrible Canal dell'Orfano; it was over the grave of my unhappy father. In the morning I was back below the Rialto Bridge. She did not come; I thought she must be angry. In the afternoon I remained below the Rialto Bridge. She did not come. Evening came. I could not wait longer, and hurried to her apartment. I asked after her. She had gone out early in the morning, and had not yet returned. I hurried to the foreigner's hotel. He had sailed in the morning for Trieste, in the company of some woman, and no one knew where he was from. I was distraught. The following morning, another boat sailed to Trieste; I joined it, in order to be taken to the other side of the Adriatic. I could not wait another day. – For the last time I was rocked in my boat in the harbour at Venice. In the morning, we sailed away; a head wind delayed us, and we reached the harbour at Trieste only on the third day. I hastened around Trieste as quickly as possible, up, down – all in vain. By evening I had heard, in response to my questions, that a foreigner answering my description had left on the highway leading to Laibach. I hastened up to the highway. At Opicina I checked my step, looking round to see which way they had turned. 'Where am I hastening? Will I overtake them? –' I asked myself aloud.

Far below me lay the gardens of Trieste and the vineyards of Opicina, and, on the hill above them, the chestnuts were in bloom. The houses of Trieste gleamed white by the sea, and beyond them the mountains stretched into the distance. Dense mists rolled from the surface of the sea, and the sun was already long bathed in it. It seemed to me that I should run down and cast myself into the bottomless depths of the quiet waters. I clasped my hands; involuntarily, I raised my right hand towards the evening sky, and a terrible oath of vengeance emerged from my mouth over the dark sea. – Once more I gazed down – and for the last time I saw the ocean; – since that time I have never seen it again!

I ran on and on, into the wide world, without purpose, without end! – At last I came upon a band of Gypsies, and to this day I wander through a strange land, far, far from my own country, despised, unknown; nothing – nothing remains to me from bygone times, save terrible memory, save the ardent desire for vengeance, nothing – nothing! –

O Venice! Venice! good night, Venice! –

A dark night, a cold night encircles me, in a desolate forest, my homeland. – My little boat! are you still rocked on the waves by the Rialto Bridge, or are you now perhaps already smashed to pieces, broken into individual timbers, out – out – in a distant ocean –? – Now I am sitting, alone, warmed by the last heat of the fire, writing this distressful letter; my companions sleep around me; above me, the pale stars grow rigid. All is asleep; – there is silence through the distant forest; only I do not sleep, I, and my memory, and my burning desire for vengeance. – When will my memory be put to rest? – When will my desire for vengeance be extinguished? –

Thus read the letter of the old Gypsy.

Now his memory has been put to rest; now his burning desire for vengeance has been extinguished. – High on the gallows, he too has fallen asleep; a deep peace has entered the breast of the hanged man. His lifeless eyes have been turned towards the south, and his head has been inclined towards the land of his birth. His pale face was serene. A light breeze – blown from the south – has caressed his grey locks.

Venice was his final thought – and a strange land will be his grave.

15

See the young man in the flower of his youth!
Scarcely has he shone in the world
than his heart becomes frozen.
Drowned in a sewer of unclean pleasures,
he dwells alone among men.

JULIAN KORSAK
A Pilgrimage (1830)

A corrupt spirit becomes oblivious,
and will perish alone.

Without hope – without being free –
he took his leave – – – – –

LUDWIK JABŁONOWSKI
Hetman Żmija (1834)

THERE WAS A SMALL level area between the low hills above the entrance to the frequently worked valley. Golden ears of ripening grain were bending across it in the light evening breeze, and their whispers – like quiet evening music, accompanying the singing of the tiny insects flying by – were cradled in a contemplative reverie over the turf covering the fresh graves of the old Jew and his daughter. Six stones on the graves, as are customary in Jewish burials, protruded from the half-dry turf on this level area, and three small trees swayed in the long shadow cast over this sorrowful earth.

The purple radiance of the setting sun was casting individual rays of red flame over the thick ears of grain on the quiet plain, and glittering clouds of mayflies were swaying over the blossoming hedges around the earth of the graveyard. – Deep silence was enveloping a deeply riven heart, and deep silence enfolding the sun's dying rays, over a realm of sorrow.

Young Valdemar – in the same attire as that he was wearing when he had first arrived in this region – was sitting, or rather lying, with his head supported by the balk at the east of this level area, with his broken musical instrument beside him, among the swaying flowers known as the Tears of the Virgin. The gleams of the departing sun dwelt on his mournful face; – but its rays did not discover a single tear in the eye of the lonely man. In events as terrible as those that had touched him in these days, his sensations had been tormented to death and extinguished; – or so it seemed. In his heart the peace of the grave, it seemed, had put his wellbeing to death.

He had bidden farewell to the first, and last, love of his life, and his grief was temperate. He was not envious of her eternal rest after the hardships of so stormy a life; for a terrible storm had cast him out also – wrecking the ship that should have brought him to the Promised Land –, he too had been cast out on an island of deep silence; – he had been elevated, lifted above all the rages and passions of human life. To contemplate his face would at this moment have calmed the storms in the breast of any still battling the waves of a stormy existence.

It seemed that grief dwelt in his handsome face only by force of habit, that sorrow had found a home in his engaging countenance only by virtue of custom; and its features were made indistinct by silence, as if covered by a veil.

His face, though young, was majestic to the highest degree at this moment. His lips were motionless; his thoughts were not given utterance, even in the merest whisper. His dark blue eyes – raised to the deep canopy of heaven – were following the small light clouds skipping like white lambs across the lovely blue of the evening sky, up to the point where it blazed in brighter colours, changing more and more, until at the edge of the grain, it joined the turf with the setting sun in a single ultramarine brilliance. It seemed to him that Leah's spirit had dissolved in her last breath and was encircling the whole globe of the earth in the azure – in the redness – of the evening sky; and that one day his spirit too would dissolve and be united with it in a divine grandeur. He sat there in this way for about half an hour; it was the final farewell.

It was impossible for him to remain in that place; whether because of what had taken place there, or whether because he was accustomed to a life of wandering, or whether for other reasons – I do not know. – He had made his will, and he had settled his affairs; and without informing anyone, he had resolved to return to wandering the wide world. He was here at Leah's graveside solely to take his leave, or to confirm his intention.

In front of the Jews' cottage below sat old Bárta, in the quiet of the evening in the beautiful dale. Judith and he had been given the Jews' cottage, which had reverted to the authorities after the deaths of the Jews. Bárta had applied for it, and – on account of the services he had rendered to the late count in battle, and also because he had been promised it, if it should revert to the authorities – he had also been granted it. He was required, however, in accordance with the wishes of the young count, to entertain every traveller who wished to stay overnight, free of charge, and a certain sum of money was to be provided annually by the castle for this purpose.

Now Bárta was sitting blissfully in front of his own cottage, his own little garden. With his glass before him, he was contemplating how he would proclaim the terrible incidents in the Napoleonic wars, in front of the Rhine, beyond it, on it, and in it, to all his new arrivals and guests; and meanwhile Judith was preparing supper over a small fire in the cottage, and coming out to him from time to time. The voice of Bárta, the storyteller, was echoing in the valley.

At that point, slow but heavy footsteps could be heard – above them, on the footpath leading around the old castle into the valley –, and some stones rolled down into the dale, through the thick bushes, with a loud clatter. No one could be seen, however, on account of the dense undergrowth around the path. Now the footsteps fell silent; the traveller must be walking on soft earth. Bárta listened.

It was silent in the distant, beautiful dale; the purple sky above him stretched from one side to the other, and in darker hues the trees cast their shadows over the rocks, and around the lake below, on whose surface the waterlilies shone white. From time to time, the song of a nightingale warbled lovingly from the dark undergrowth by the stream, and the cry of a lonely cuckoo echoed monotonously from the rocks opposite, where birches wept, bending above the roofs of the desolate city. Wisps of smoke drifted over the cottages, small fires glowed through their open doors, and the herdsmen were singing as they drove their flocks into their quiet folds.

Bárta listened. Footsteps could now be heard in the vale below the cottage, – now on the footbridge over the stream; still no one could be seen for the dense undergrowth. Bárta wanted to call out, supposing that some traveller had inadvertently missed the only inn – his inn. Just then, however, an indistinct figure appeared, walking on the path, from cottage to cottage, up the hill on the other side; from time to time it disappeared behind the looming rocks; from time to time it reappeared, as it passed the doors of the low cottages, obscuring their small fires.

'Judith! Judith!' cried Bárta. She came running. 'Look, is not that our young lord there – on my word – dressed like a Gypsy?' cried Bárta. 'Yes, dressed like a Gypsy! aye, aye – what? who would dare? –' Raising her hand to her brow, Judith shielded her eyes, and looked over to the path on the other side. Yes – it is he, young Valdemar, count of Bork, – now again he has passed beyond the last of the cottages, with his head bowed. Slowly he is climbing higher and higher.

Now he is up the hill. – He has not looked back at his native land; he is going far – far away. –

Around him lie blossoming meadows, fertile fields, azure forests, his homeland, his inheritance. The dark mountains in the distance – rolling, like ghastly pale waves, up to the rose-coloured sky and to clouds that are as if bloodstained – have bidden the lonely pilgrim farewell. He sees nothing; he is going away – farther – farther.

The long road stretches across the plain; far – far, into the distance – like a blind river – it falls into the dark mountains. On it, he is going far – far away.

The young Gypsy has departed into the wide world. May God go with him!

RECENT TITLES PUBLISHED BY JANTAR

And My Head Exploded: Tales of Desire, Delirium and Decadence from Fin-de-Siècle Prague

Translated by Geoffrey Chew, with an introduction by Peter Zusi

TEN TALES: JULIUS ZEYER: *Inultus: A Prague Legend* (1892); BOŽENA BENEŠOVÁ: *Tale for All Souls' Day* (1902) and *In the Twilight* (1900); MILOŠ MARTEN: *Cortigiana* (*The Courtesan*, 1911); ARTHUR BREISKY: *Prose Poem, after Félicien Rops,* Mors syphilitica (1909) and *Confession of a Graphomaniac* (1909); JULIUS ZEYER: *El Cristo de la Luz: A Toledo Legend* (1892); JIŘÍ KARÁSEK ZE LVOVIC: *The Legend of Simon Magus* (1911); FRANTIŠEK GELLNER: *My Travelling Companion* (1912); RICHARD WEINER: *The Empty Chair: An Analysis of an Unwritten Tale* (1917)

-- ISBN: 978-0-9934467-1-7

Gaudeamus *by* RICHARD

Translated by David Short

"All crimes, great and small, finally lead to murder."

Based on real events.

The unloved wife of a doctor practising in Slovakia comes across his medical notes after his death. One 'unofficial patient' has severe problems coming to terms with the disappearance and murder of his childhood sweetheart. Set in Slovakia from the mid-1970s onwards, historical fact, murder, loss and mourning combine delicately in a tale of love, loss, redemption and joy.

-- ISBN: 978-0-9933773-4-1

Three Plastic Rooms *by* PETRA HŮLOVÁ

Translated by Alex Zucker, with an introduction by Peter Zusi

A foul-mouthed Prague prostitute muses on her profession, aging and the nature of materialism. She explains her world view in the scripts and commentaries of her own reality TV series combining the mundane with fetishism, violence, wit and an unvarnished mixture of vulgar and poetic language.

-- ISBN: 978-0-9933773-9-6

For further news on new books and events, please visit
www.JantarPublishing.com